Closing the Circle:
Narratives of a Nonagenarian

A second collection of short stories by Anne "Bunty" Loucks

Closing the Circle:

Narratives of a Nonagenarian

"For the unlearned, old age is winter, for the learned, it is the harvest." The Talmud

"We are always the same inside." Gertrude Stein

"Large streams from little fountains flow; tall oaks from little acorns grow." D. Everett

A second collection of short stories by Anne "Bunty" Loucks

Cover Illustrations

"Fashions in Britain Through the Ages: From the Caveman to the Present Day"

by
Nancy Patrick
©1962

The front cover illustrations were drawn by Nancy Patrick when she was twelve years old as a grade seven history project, "Fashions in Britain Through the Ages: From the Caveman to the Present Day." With the naïveté of youth, Nancy was undaunted by the scope of such a project!

Back cover photographs: Bunty in November 2012 at the book signing of her first book; Bunty as an actress, age 18; a young mother, age 27; and a mother of four, age 32.

ISBN: 978-0-9966113-1-2

Cover design by Taylor Whitney
Cover illustrations by Nancy Patrick
Page layout and design by Taylor Whitney
Assistant graphic design by Michael Sikora
Back cover photograph by Taylor Whitney, 2012
Back cover photographs from the Patrick Family Collection

For additional copies, please contact
info@preservethepast.com or spatrick@ryerson.ca
lulu.com | barnesandnoble.com | amazon.com

PTP Publishing
a division of Preserving The Past, LLC
Toronto, Ontario
Rochester, New York
Los Angeles, California
www.preservethepast.com

PRESERVING THE PAST

Dedication

Closing the Circle: Narratives of a Nonagenarian is dedicated to my four daughters, Wendy, Barbara, Nancy and Susy, for their love and support over the years.

Acknowledgements

 [ornamental flourish]

Thank you to my son-in-law, John Raiswell, and my daughters Barbara, Nancy and Susy, for their time, knowledge and assistance in helping me complete this new collection of stories.

I am extremely grateful to Taylor Whitney for her professional, skillful and creative approach in designing this book and to her company PTP Publishing, a division of Preserving The Past, LLC, for publishing *Closing the Circle: Narratives of a Nonagenarian*.

Thank you to my daughter Nancy, also, for providing the cover artwork (drawn when she was just twelve years old) that illustrates the type of characters and the eras in which in the stories are set.

Bunty Loucks

Introduction

For as long as we can remember, our mother's mind was full of stories, but it wasn't until she turned ninety that she felt perhaps the time had come to start considering them for publication.

Bunty grew up in Montreal, and her experiences at McGill University during the formative war years, and as a mother of four daughters in the 1950s and 1960s, provided her with a rich background for the stories in this new collection. Her move to rural Ontario later in life added more grist for the literary mill, with inspiration from the many people with whom she crossed paths.

Growing up with Bunty as our mother meant lots of wholesome meals and a never-ending circle of guests at our dinner table...for while meat and potatoes may have fed our bodies, it was people and their stories that fed our minds. From soup to nuts, our Sunday dinners had it all.

As with her earlier collection, "Flotsam and Jetsam: Chronicles of Colourful Characters I Have Known," most of the stories are based in a kernel of fact, with some kernels being larger than others. All are burnished by memory and imagination.

Love found and lost in the intensity of war time, unwanted pregnancies, the comic and tragic foibles of human nature—these were the common themes in the lives of people she encountered. Now our mother's own life has come full circle, but we can hear her voice in these stories, offering an appealing glimpse into the social mores of the twentieth century—a world that is gradually fading into history.

Barbara Patrick, Nancy Kellett and Susan Patrick

Table of Contents

A Blot on the Escutcheon

It is almost impossible to exaggerate the magnitude of the shock waves that engulfed the small town of Brockston when, in May 1919, on the eve of her wedding, Eleanor Fleming suddenly eloped with the best man, whose acquaintance she had made only a few days before.

Her parents found this note on her pillow the next morning:

> Dear Mother and Father,
> I hope you can find it in your hearts to forgive me. It is hard for me to put my feelings on paper, but I feel I am more vibrantly alive since meeting Randolph than I have ever felt in my whole life. It would be wrong for me to marry Lester. Randolph and I plan to be married in New York State as soon as possible and I will be in touch shortly. Please try not to worry. I am so happy.
>
> With love,
> Eleanor

A few weeks later, a chastened Eleanor returned home, still not married, but sadder, wiser and pregnant. It happened that the Flemings were related to everybody who was anybody in town, and news of the illegitimate pregnancy would be a disgrace of major proportions. It was of paramount importance to the whole family that the situation be handled in such a way that it would not be a permanent blight on the family tree.

Under a cloak of secrecy, Eleanor was hustled off to an aunt in Edmonton, where she remained until the baby, a girl who was christened Flora, was born. They stayed on for a year until it was deemed safe to return to Brockston with a carefully crafted story about a failed marriage.

Flora and her mother lived sometimes with Eleanor's parents, and sometimes with other relatives, until eventually Eleanor did marry.

From the outset, Flora was a rebel, and no one was able to control her. She did not get along well with her mother or step-father, and after a short time, she was dispatched to boarding school, where she established a reputation as a non-conformist and trouble-maker. Flora had always been curious about the identity of her father and one day confronted her grandmother, demanding to be told the truth about her birth. She threatened otherwise to make up a story and spread scandalous rumours. Her grandmother agreed on the condition that Flora would never attempt to contact him.

Flora was fascinated by the story, especially after discovering that her father was a well-known architect in New York, and his picture often appeared in the newspaper. Just recently, in fact, Flora had heard him interviewed in a national radio broadcast.

On the pretext of taking a course in Fine Arts, she went to New York and immediately telephoned her father, despite her promise to her grandmother. He sounded delighted to hear from her and suggested they have lunch together that day. They spent several hours at a fashionable restaurant, in animated conversation. Flora was as enchanted by her father as he appeared to be with her. They parted with the understanding that he would be in touch in a day or two. Flora was ecstatic and immediately began to make plans to change her last name to his.

However, she never heard from her father again. Her telephone calls and then letters to him remained unanswered. Her dream world evaporated and the pain of that rejection affected her whole life thereafter. She seemed detached and unable to relate to other people. She was like a ship without an anchor, drifting from one unhappy affair to another.

By now, it was 1939. Flora was nineteen years old and the Second World War had just begun. The whole world seemed to be on the move. She went overseas with a troupe that provided entertainment for servicemen, and was notorious for her outrageous performances and risqué dancing. Her *pièce de résistance* was her singing of Kurt Weill and Ira Gershwin's song "The Saga of Jenny," clad in a flimsy negligee. She delighted in belting out the lines that always brought down the house.

> *Jenny made her mind up at seventy-five*
> *She would live to be the oldest woman alive.*
> *But gin and rum and destiny play funny tricks,*
> *And poor Jenny kicked the bucket at seventy-six*

One evening in a bar in London, she met a young man from her hometown of Brockston and got into conversation. He appeared to be in low spirits and was attempting to drown his sorrow in beer. He told Flora, "I just got word that my father has died."

"I'm sorry," she replied.

"Don't be," he said. "I'm not. I hated him. I know this sounds incredible, but his first fiancée walked out on him on the evening before the wedding—ran off with his best man. He just never got over her..." He talked about how his parents' marriage had been a fiasco. His father had married in haste on the rebound.

"His bitterness made our family life a misery. He broke my mother's heart. He was infatuated with this other woman. He never loved my mother or me." Her companion took another swig of beer, and said, "I bet I'm the only guy you've ever met whose life was ruined before it even began, all because my old man was jilted at the altar." An idea was forming in Flora's mind.

"What did you say your name was?"

At the reply, Flora stared at him in shocked amazement for a few moments, but did not speak.

"And you're from Brockston? Well, well, well, what a

coincidence," she said at last. "Guess whose old lady it was who dumped your father? You're not the only one whose life was messed up. My mother ruined my life too, but there's not much we can do about it now, is there? So let's drink a toast to them. Bottoms up, down the hatch, and so's your old man, chum! To hell with both of them." They clinked glasses.

Author's note: "Flora" died recently (2013), at age 93. Her life had not been a happy one.

A Tide in the Affairs of Men

Ⓢ

It is a self-evident truth that war is a disrupting factor, and for those of my generation, there were very few whose lives were not changed in one way or another by the Second World War. Some stories ended happily, some tragically. In many cases, people whose lives, under any other circumstances, would never have intersected, were thrown together quite by fate. With the intensity of the war, when life was so uncertain, and death a strong possibility, people often grasped at momentary happiness without thought for the future.

Looking back across a span of over seventy years, I remember one of the most poignant stories was that of my friend Elizabeth. Early in the war, Elizabeth's mother received a letter from an old school friend, Grace, in England. She wrote to say that her son, Richard, would be in Montreal for a day or two before travelling out west to train as a pilot under the Commonwealth Air Training Plan, and asked if he might call on them. Elizabeth's mother wrote back immediately, inviting Richard to come and stay as long as he wished.

A few weeks later, Richard arrived as expected and was invited to dinner that evening. Early the next morning, I received a telephone call from Elizabeth. "You're not going believe this," she said, "but last night, I met the man I would like to marry."

"That's very sudden," I replied. "How do you know?"

"From the moment I met him, I had the feeling we were destined to be together. I can't explain it, but I've never been more certain of anything in my life."

They only had that one evening together, as Richard left the next morning for Elementary Flying Training School in High River, Alberta.

The two corresponded during the seven-to-eight months he spent in training, exchanging letters almost daily. Later, Elizabeth showed me the letter she received from him

> *I have lived most of my entire life of 24 years and 3 months without even knowing you existed. How can it be now that I cannot imagine life without you? You have bewitched me. Dare I hope that you are as drawn to me as I am to you?*

Elizabeth kept that letter close to her heart for the rest of her life.

After graduating with his pilot's wings, Richard wrote to say that he was being sent back to England and expected to have a brief leave in Halifax before embarking. He asked Elizabeth to meet him there and marry him. Her answer to both questions was an enthusiastic "Yes." Despite the misgivings of her parents about the marriage, since she had not known Richard for very long, Elizabeth was quite certain that they would be happy together.

She and her parents travelled to Halifax and the marriage duly took place. Richard and Elizabeth had hoped to have at least a few days together, but he was ordered to leave the day after the wedding. As soon as Elizabeth returned to Montreal, she put the wheels in motion to get permission to go to England, where she planned to live near Richard's RAF base. Getting permission to go overseas was not an easy matter during the war, and it was only possible because Elizabeth had been born in England. The government bureaucracy moved slowly and the months hung heavily, until finally the papers arrived.

I still vividly remember the farewell party the night before Elizabeth left, and the excitement she felt in anticipating her new life. However, her future was not to be as she envisaged it. Fate intervened.

Awaiting Elizabeth's imminent arrival, Richard had gone to stay with his mother in Liverpool. The night before the ship docked, however, there was a massive air raid, in which Richard was killed. His mother lived, but was trapped in the rubble of her house. Eventually an air raid warden found and freed her. Apart from her bruises, and other minor injuries, she was almost unhurt physically, but was inconsolable to learn of the loss of her son.

By chance, the air raid warden had with him two little boys whose parents had both been killed in the same air raid. Thinking to console her, and at the same time to help the boys, the air raid warden asked Grace if she would look after them for the rest of the night. Grace agreed, and the warden helped her and the boys to a nearby air raid shelter, where they were given hot drinks and were settled down for the rest of the night. The boys cried for their mother almost incessantly. They clung to Grace and, putting aside her own grief, she did her best to comfort them. In the morning, the authorities began their search for the boys' relatives.

Grace, with the boys, met Elizabeth when she arrived in Liverpool and gave her the dreadful news of Richard's death. Elizabeth was devastated. She felt there was now no point in remaining in England and she planned to return to Canada as soon as possible. Until her return could be arranged, she stayed with her mother-in-law and the boys in the temporary accommodation that had been found for them. As time passed and no relatives were found, Grace continued to care for the boys and found real comfort in this. As the effects of her shock started to dull somewhat, Elizabeth, too, found comfort in being with Grace and talking to her about Richard. Indeed, she felt that her mother-in-law, who had now lost three sons to the war, was the only person who could share her intense grief. This, and the need to provide a home for the orphans, created a bond between the two women. Elizabeth gave up her plan to travel back to Canada and made her home with Grace and the boys. They all lived together happily and, in time, Grace officially adopted the children, whom she and Elizabeth grew to love as their own family. Elizabeth had a successful career as a magazine writer, and never remarried.

Grace has now died, but I keep in touch with Elizabeth. The boys are, of course, now middle-aged men and have children (and even grandchildren) of their own, and she is still very much part of the family. So, after all, her life was happy and fulfilled. To her credit, Elizabeth "had taken the current when it served" and it did "lead on to fortune," but not in the way that she had expected.

MacDonald and MacDougall

Following the outbreak of war in 1939, Archie MacDonald, a native of Aberdeen who was then working as a rubber planter in Malaya, joined the British Army. During basic training in England, he became friends with Hector MacDougall, a Glasgow accountant. Successfully completing their course, both were recommended for Officers' Training. On graduation day, all spit and polish, they were paraded before the Brigadier, whose name was Bustard. MacDonald went in first.

"Good show, MacDonald!" puffed the Brigadier in his best Colonel Blimp voice. "In which theatre of operations would you like to serve?"

"Sir," replied MacDonald, "I've spent seven years in the Far East. I'm used to the climate. I speak several native dialects. I'm single. I'm happy to go wherever I'm most useful."

"Well!" snorted the Brigadier. "I daresay we'd all enjoy lolling about in the tropics, MacDonald, and travelling around at Government expense, wouldn't we?"

Before one could say, "Brigadier Bustard's a bastard," MacDonald found himself aboard a troop train bound for Birmingham to be stationed there for the duration.

MacDougall went in next.

"Well done, MacDougall! And where might you like to serve?"

"Sir," responded MacDougall, "my wife is expecting twins, and we've two other small children. If possible, I would hope to remain in Britain for a bit."

"Doubtless you would," barked the Brigadier, bristling, "but there's a war on, you know, MacDougall! We can't all stay home, can we?"

MacDougall, bag and baggage, was soon aboard a boat bound for Bombay.

Moral: When dealing with bureaucracy, it's best to save your breath to cool your porridge.

Waltzing Matilda

I cannot vouch for the absolute accuracy of every detail of this story, because it happened a very long time ago, and my memory is not as good as it once was. However, this is essentially what took place.

The first contingent of Royal Australian Air Force personnel taking part in the newly-formed British Commonwealth Air Training Plan arrived in Montreal on a cold winter's day in 1942. They had come to Vancouver by sea from Australia, and had immediately boarded a train, taking them 3,000 miles across the country heading for their next destination—the manning depot in Lachine, Quebec. When the train pulled into Windsor Station in Montreal, the Aussies disembarked with all their gear, dumped it on the platform, and sat down on their luggage. A Royal Canadian Air Force officer approached them. "Who is in charge?" he demanded. No one seemed to know. He finally found a sergeant and tried to get the men on their feet and moving, but to no avail. The officer told them that a Wing Commander was waiting to deliver a speech welcoming them to Canada, and the band was at the ready to strike up "Waltzing Matilda." No one moved a muscle. Finally, the sergeant got to his feet and announced that they were not going anywhere until they found their mascot, a joey (baby kangaroo), they had brought all the way from Australia with them, and who had leapt off the train and escaped just as the train slowed down to enter the station. There was a palaver between the RCAF brass and the Australian sergeant, who had to halt the conversation every few minutes to consult with his mates. They were demanding a 24-hour leave to search for "Joey," who was in danger of perishing in the rigours of the Canadian winter. Because there seemed to be no other solution, this was agreed to.

The airmen checked their dunnage bags and belongings, and agreed to return to the station in 24 hours. They set off straight away to search for Joey. It was reported

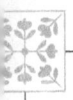

that they searched high and low all over Montreal, but I believe they made sure to include every bar, tavern and nightclub in town. The public rallied to the cause. Reports were telephoned in to local radio stations telling of sightings of the lost Joey — on the south shore, in the Laurentians, even as far away as Cornwall, beyond the Ontario border. There were hourly bulletins on the news, but in vain. There was no finding him.

The Aussies returned to the station the next day, as promised, but refused to return to duty until they could spend another 24 hours on the search. Enthusiasm restored, they revisited all the previous day's haunts, and left no stone unturned in the seedier parts of Montreal in their efforts to locate the elusive kangaroo. At the end of their second 24-hour leave, with no Joey in hand, they returned to the station, collected their gear and announced reluctantly that they were ready to report to the manning depot, minus their mascot. No one ever admitted it, of course, but rumour was rife in certain quarters in Montreal that Joey never existed. The whole plot had been concocted as a way for them to get leave and let off steam after a few weeks at sea, followed by a week cooped up on a troop train. But the legend was such that for years afterwards, members of the populace would tell of seeing a kangaroo in an RAAF cap at a rakish angle on his head in their back gardens.

The Pleasure of Your Company

⌒

In the dark days of the Second World War, in 1942, when the news was bleak and the outcome uncertain, the one thing that kept the MacIntyre family going was the elaborate planning for Granny MacIntyre's 100th birthday. The family lived in the small coastal fishing village of Lossiemouth in the north of Scotland, not far from Elgin. The only other excitement in the town was the encampment of Polish soldiers, who had arrived in 1940, to help defend Britain against the threat of invasion through Scotland from German troops stationed in Norway.

The war rationing of food was severe, and the family had been saving up their coupons for months to buy the ingredients for a cake, a rare treat that none of them had tasted since the beginning of the war. As it happened, British government newsreels of the time featured short films encouraging the consumption of potatoes and carrots—crops that were plentiful, as opposed to wheat—which was in short supply. The family decided to spin out their rations by trying a new recipe being promoted—carrot cake. In addition, they had been saving the tea bags that relatives in Canada had been sending.

The MacIntyres had recently made the acquaintance of Captain Jarrick Wolofsky, a company commander in the Polish army, and had opened their home to him, inviting him to stop by any time. He was a lonely young man, and he was glad to be accepted by them. His English was not good, and their Polish non-existent, so communication was often difficult, but despite this, a strong friendship developed between the family and him. After a long discussion, they decided to include Jarrick in the family party.

With great care, Jennie MacIntyre, the granddaughter, who prided herself on her penmanship, crafted the seventeen formal invitations in her finest script.

> *Hamish MacIntyre & family*
> *request the pleasure of your company*
> *to celebrate the 100th birthday*
> *of Elspeth MacIntyre*
> *at 3:00 pm on June 10th*
> *at Stotfield Cottage.*

On the day of the party, the cake was ready, large enough to provide one tiny square for each person, with one large candle sufficing for the one hundred. The refreshments were barely adequate for the numbers, but everybody had made such sacrifices to contribute to the food that there was still a festive air about. The kettle was whistling on the wood stove, when a strange sound was heard—the sound of marching feet on the hard surface of the road getting louder and louder, as if approaching the cottage. At the head of a group of about a dozen marching soldiers was Captain Wolofsky. He halted his men in front of the cottage and stepped forward to greet the McIntyres with a formal speech. "I am thanking you for your invitation for my company. Too bad only a few can come today. The others, they are on duty. I hope you are not offended." There was consternation among the family members at this unexpected turn of events, and it was Jennie who realized the nature of the misunderstanding. It was the wording on the invitation! However, with true Scots hospitality, she greeted the soldiers warmly, meanwhile adding more water to the teapot and cutting the cake into ever-smaller pieces. In the end, the party was a great success, aided no doubt by the home-made vodka brought by the Polish soldiers.

The story had an unexpected ending, as young Jennie and Jarrick fell in love, were married a few months later, and as far as we know, lived happily-ever-after in Lossiemouth.

To this day, some seventy odd years later, in that part of Scotland, I am told, one can still find, amongst the MacPhersons, McGillavrys and MacIntyres, wee red-haired bairns, speaking in a fine Scottish burr, answering to the name Wolofsky.

Greenshields' D-Day AWOL Adventure

Lorne Greenshields was a Canadian who joined the Army at the outbreak of the Second World War, and was duly sent overseas. On D-Day, a detachment of his regiment, 33 men and 3 officers, crossed the channel on a small ship. As they neared the French coast, they transferred to a Landing Craft Infantry (LCI). Unbeknownst to them, the Germans had installed underwater steel barriers, rigged with explosives, along the shore. As the LCI approached land, it hit one of the barriers, and there was a huge explosion.

When Lorne regained consciousness, he found he was back on board the small ship that had carried them across the channel, stark naked and with no identification. Of the rest of his group, there was no sign. Wrapped in a blanket found amongst the ship's supplies, he was taken back to England as the ship returned home. Greenshields, being in a state of shock, was unable to provide any information about what had happened, and because he had no ID, the authorities had him under suspicion as a possible enemy spy. He was sent inland, away from the shore, where he might have proved a danger, and in the chaos, obtained a uniform of sorts, a complete kit, and left to cope on his own.

Within a few days, he somehow managed to hitch-hike back to the coast and found a British Colonel who was in charge of dispatching reinforcement troops across the channel. "My name is Lorne Greenshields, sir," he told the Colonel. "I am a trained Canadian Reconnaissance Officer, and I want to rejoin my unit in France. However, I was torpedoed on D-Day, so I have no identification or papers."

"Go away," said the Colonel testily. "If you don't have papers, you don't exist. I don't have time to worry about you. Get lost!"

Lorne returned to see the Colonel every day for a week, and finally, to get rid of him, the Colonel said, "There's a

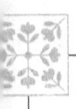

Canadian Major about a mile down the beach. Go and see him. Perhaps he can help you."

Lorne duly found the Major, who, on learning that Lorne had no papers, said predictably, "If you don't have papers, you don't exist. You could be anybody. You could be Hitler's butler, for all I know."

Lorne persisted, and when the Major learned that he was from Montreal, he relented a bit, asking where Lorne had lived, what school he had attended, and the name of the principal. They discovered that they had mutual friends and acquaintances. "I guess you're okay," said the Major. He telephoned the British Colonel who had referred Lorne to him, explained the situation, and asked what he should do.

"I don't care what the @#$% you do with him!" the Colonel bellowed. "I told him that he doesn't exist, and now I'm telling you." He hung up.

The Canadian Major was beginning to see there was a problem. However, he found Lorne a tent to sleep in, and Lorne was drowsing on the floor when he heard the sound of the many marching feet of a large group of soldiers approaching. He pulled the tent flap over and saw them "falling in" with full marching order kit. He went looking for the Major and asked where they were going.

"Oh," said the Major, "that's the draft for France leaving tonight."

"What would happen if I fell in with them?" asked Lorne. "You can't," said the Major in an exasperated tone, "you don't exist!"

Lorne grabbed his kit and fell in with the draft. By the next morning he was safely in France. He approached the first Canadian unit he spotted and asked a sergeant, "How do I get in touch with the 7th Recce?"

"I'll get them on the phone for you," replied the obliging sergeant. A minute later, the call was through. Lorne asked to speak to the Colonel of his regiment.

When the Colonel came on the line, Lorne said "Greenshields here, sir."

The Colonel bellowed back, "Greenshields! Where the hell have you been for the last ten days? Trying to shirk your duty? There's a war on, you know. Get back here on the double." At that, Lorne knew he was home.

Author's note: 7th Recce is the 7th Canadian Reconnaissance Regiment.

A Soap Opera Saga in Three Acts

Act One: Montreal, May 1943

"Daddy," sobbed Diana, wiping the tears from her eyes, "I know you think this is just some silly, romantic fantasy I've dreamed up, and that I'll get over it, but...Blake and I are soulmates! I knew the moment I first saw him that day at the post office, on my birthday, when he found my wallet, that I had met my destiny in life. I can't tell you how I knew; I just did. It was as though I recognized Blake on sight as someone I had known and loved in a previous existence, and he told me later he had that same feeling. He said he felt magnetized by me. Then, when I discovered it was *his* birthday, too, that very day, April 24th, which of course was also Mummy's birthday—and the anniversary of her death—I knew for certain that our meeting had been pre-ordained. I didn't even discover until later that his mother had died the day he was born. Our meeting couldn't possibly have happened purely by chance. There were just... too many... strange coincidences." She paused for a moment to reach for another tissue to mop her eyes.

"All my life, Daddy," she continued, still sobbing, "you and I have been so attuned to each other. You can almost read my mind, so why... can't you see that Blake and I were destined... before we were even born, to meet, fall in love, get married, and be together always? We love... each other, and we always will, and we... just want to get married... before he's shipped... overseas." Her tears began to flow again, and coursed down her cheeks in little rivulets.

Her father, Roger, reached across the kitchen table and took both her hands in his. "Diana, dear," he said gently, "I know how you feel. I do, honestly! I just wish I could get you to see the situation from my point of view. Let's look at the facts again, shall we? First of all, you're barely sixteen. You're still at school, and you have another year after this. How old is Blake? Eighteen? How long have you known each other? Less

than a month! You're both far too young to make such an important decision. If, as you say, you're soul mates, meant for each other, then it will all happen in the fullness of time. If it's meant to be, it will be. When the war is over, and you're both mature enough to know your own minds, then we–"

"But, Daddy," interrupted Diana, dabbing at her tear-stained face with a wadded-up tissue, and almost unable to get her words out, "I don't know why I can't... make you see... things from our point of view. I realize you're doing... what you think is right, and what is best... for me, but you... just don't... seem to understand, Daddy," she said sadly, slowly shaking her head from side to side, as her tears continued to flow.

"I understand a great deal better than you think I do, my darling," her father replied. "I understand, because I've been there! I was sixteen myself once upon a time, you know, and I remember only too well how I felt the first time I fell in love. Her name was Holly, and we were so head-over-heels in love, we thought we'd die if we couldn't spend the rest of our lives together. Three months later, we were both going steady with someone else, and no longer even on speaking terms with one another. I can't even remember her last name now!"

Diana's sobs continued unabated. She gave no indication that she had even heard her father's words. Her shoulders heaved, and her breath came in short gasps. "You know a lot... of important people, Daddy, lawyers and judges. Perhaps... we could be married by... special license or something."

"Look, dear," her father said gently, as he handed her the box of tissues, "the one thing I want most in this world is for you to be happy, but that being said, I am legally and morally responsible for your welfare. I would be derelict in my duty as a parent if I were to give my consent to your marriage at the age of sixteen. It's out of the question, dear! I like Blake, and from what I have seen of him, he is a fine young man, but you have only known each other for about five minutes. All

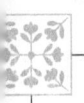

you've told me about him is that he grew up on a farm in Saskatchewan, that he's just completed training as a pilot in the RCAF, and that he's on embarkation leave. We know nothing at all about his family, or his background. Trust me, dear, one day you'll thank me for putting the brakes on."

"No, Daddy, no!" Diana cried vehemently, between heart-rending sobs. "If I live... to be a hundred... years old, I will... never, never, never stop... loving Blake. I'll love him forever!"

"Forever is a long time, dear, and none of us can see into the future. I'm asking you to trust my judgment in this. You know you can trust me. I suppose it's because you grew up without a mother that there's a special bond between us. We've never really talked about it, but I think we're both aware it exists."

He paused for a moment as if uncertain whether or not to continue the conversation. "Diana, your happiness and welfare are the most important considerations in my life, and I love you more than you can possibly imagine. You've brought nothing but joy into my life. From the day you were born, the day that your mother died, I've tried to be both father and mother to you. I made a lot of mistakes along the way, but I had to learn on the job, so to speak, and I had no one to teach me. Losing your mother was devastating. I lost not only my wife, I lost my best friend as well. I was a twenty-one year old kid, who knew less than nothing about babies, who suddenly found himself sole caregiver to a tiny, five-pound little person, small enough to hold in the palm of my hand. It was a terrifying situation to find myself in. I was a virtual stranger in Montreal, with no friends, few acquaintances, and very little money.

"That first year was a living nightmare, but it turned out to be a coming-of-age year for me, the year I finally grew up. You were ten days old when I brought you home from the hospital, along with a little pamphlet covering the care and feeding of infants. Every morning I had to get up, make your formula, get you washed, dressed and fed, have my own breakfast, take you across town by streetcar to the nursery centre, and be at my job by 8:30. At the end of the day, I had to reverse the process; collect you, take you home by streetcar, bath you, feed you, try to get you to sleep, and then have something to eat myself. After that, I had to wash the diapers and other things, by hand of course, since people didn't have washing machines in those days, and hang everything in the kitchen to dry overnight. Then there were the night feedings, at roughly 10:00 pm and 2:00 am. On Saturdays, I only had to work till one o'clock, so on the way home from the nursery, we did the grocery shopping, as the stores were all closed on Sundays. Luckily for me, you were a good baby. After only about three months you started sleeping through the night. It was almost as if you knew how inept I was at the job, and tried to do everything you possibly could to make things easier for me.

"It was a tough year, and I lived in constant fear that some over-zealous social worker would have me declared an incompetent parent, and try to take you away from me. The Family Welfare Supervisor had already suggested that, in her opinion, you'd be better off in foster care. I was determined not to let that happen. No one was going to take you away from me. You were your mother's parting gift to me, and I was ready to fight the whole world to keep you.

"What kept me going that year was the fact that, from the time you were about six months old, at the end of every day when I came to collect you, the moment you saw me, your little face would instantly light up in recognition, and you'd smile and squirm and wriggle and hold out your arms for me to pick you up. I can't tell you how heart-warming it was for me to feel that I mattered to someone, and that someone was actually glad to see me. All the staff at the nursery used to comment on your reaction, and gradually it dawned on me that when I left you there in the morning, you waited all day long, every day, for the moment when I would come back to get you and take you home with me. During that year, we forged an

unbreakable bond. Until Mrs. Ogilvie came into our lives, there were only the two of us in our little world, and looking back, I realize I was at least as dependent on you as you were on me. It was a symbiotic relationship, or perhaps there was some kind of mental osmosis between us."

"There is, Daddy, and that's why I was… so sure you… would understand how I feel," Diana sobbed brokenly.

"It's not a matter of understanding, dear," her father interrupted, "it's a matter of practical common sense. You are simply too young to make such a serious decision about your future. I simply cannot, in all conscience, give my consent. However, that being said, I'll make you a solemn promise that if, when the war is over, you both feel the same way about each other as you do now, you will have my whole-hearted blessing. Meanwhile, you can write back and forth and really get to know one another. Well, it's been a long day, and I'm rather tired, so I'll say good night. Cheer up, dear. Remember, the war can't last forever, you know."

The next morning, before leaving for school, Diana relayed the gist of this conversation with her father to Blake over the telephone. "I couldn't persuade him to change his mind, Blake," she said sadly. "The only person who might have been able to do that is his friend, Lorna, and she is out of town till next week. I know she would have understood."

In the end they made a pact that, since there was now no chance of being married before Blake's leave ended, they would make the most of whatever time they had together, and live only for the moment, giving no thought to what might lie ahead.

Her father made a point of having a few quiet words alone with Blake when he came for dinner later that day. "I hope Diana has told you that I have nothing whatsoever against you personally, Blake. The fact is I know very little about you, but what I do know, I like, and I admire and respect you. Canada is fortunate to have young men of your calibre ready to risk their lives to defend our freedom. Personally, I find the very concept of flying intimidating enough, but the idea of actually piloting a flimsy little Spitfire fighter plane, or one of those huge Lancaster bombers, loaded with hundreds of pounds of high explosives, absolutely terrifying. It must be particularly so when a lot of other guys in enemy planes are taking pot-shots at you with machine guns. That takes guts, and I salute you and your comrades."

Blake grinned sheepishly. "Well, sir, I think most people are scared skinny of flying at first. I know I was, but once you learn how to take off and land, it's so exhilarating you forget to be scared. Ever since I was a kid, I've loved wheels, anything with wheels, kiddy-cars, roller-skates, scooters, tricycles, bicycles. When I was old enough, I just couldn't wait to get my driver's license. I was so proud when I finally got it, but, you know what? My father just couldn't bring himself to trust me with the keys of the family car, unless he was in it with me. It's funny how parents, or fathers anyway, just never believe their sons will grow up and eventually become responsible adults. My father still can't believe that the Air Force actually trusts someone like me at the controls of an aircraft worth hundreds of thousands of dollars. He shakes his head in disbelief every time he thinks about it."

"Well," Diana's father replied, with a rueful half-smile, "It's hard for parents to let go of their children. It's only natural for young people to want to leave the nest, of course, but sometimes they take off before they've learned how to fly on their own. In my case, Blake, it's particularly hard for me to face the prospect of letting Diana go. Perhaps because of growing up without a mother, she and I have had a very close relationship since the day she was born.

"How we survived that first year of her life I don't know, but somehow we did. It was a case of sink or swim, and by hanging on to each other for dear life, we just managed to keep our heads above water. My father and step-mother lived in Vancouver, and Diana's mother's family lived in Sweden. There was no one I could turn to for help or advice. Diana doesn't remember, thank God, how bleak life was before we had the great good fortune to meet up with Mrs. Ogilvie, about whom I'm sure she's already told you. It was just by sheer luck that we got to know her. Diana was about a year old at the time, and we happened to stand directly behind her in a long line-up for the streetcar. Mrs. Ogilvie always said she fell in love with Diana at first sight. Somehow she and I struck up a conversation, which blossomed into a friendship, and a few weeks after that she agreed, in return for room and board, to move in with us and look after Diana. Actually, she looked after both of us. She was truly a godsend; a mother, grandmother and fairy godmother all rolled into one. She sewed all Diana's clothes, knitted sweaters, socks and mitts for both of us, and could make a dollar stretch further than anyone I've ever known. I honestly don't think we would have made it without her, and we were truly blessed to have had her with us for fourteen years.

"To get back to my reluctance to let Diana go, I always knew, of course, the day would come when I would no longer be the number one person in her life, but I just didn't expect it would come so soon. However, knowing something is one thing, but accepting it is quite another, so I hope you'll cut me some slack if I am overly protective of her."

"I will, sir, and thank you for your vote of confidence in me. It means more than I can tell you. I'll always love Diana, and I promise that when we do get married, I'll take as good care of her as you have done. It's hard to believe that a month ago I didn't know she existed, and now I can't even imagine my life without her."

The last full day Diana and Blake had together was a Saturday, one of those matchless late spring days for which Montreal is justly famous. The magnificent old elm trees, which grace both sides of Sherbrooke Street as far as the eye can see, were in full leaf.

On a clear, cloudless morning they climbed, hand in hand, to the look-out atop Mount Royal, and, as Jacques

Cartier had done some four hundred years earlier, saw spread out before them the majestic St. Lawrence River on its long journey to the Atlantic Ocean. In the distance, on the south shore, rose Mont Ste. Hilaire, a leafy forest of greenery. Blake, accustomed to the flat, treeless terrain of the prairies, was astounded by the richness and variety of the Quebec landscape, so much so, that to Diana's delight, he expressed a wish to make their home in Montreal after they were married. They ate their picnic lunch sitting on a bench near Beaver Lake, before taking a ride in a horse-drawn calèche eastward along Sherbrooke Street, and then south to 'Old Montreal.' They strolled around Place d'Armes, had supper at Scott's restaurant on Ste. Catherine Street, and afterwards attended an open-air symphony concert under the stars at McGill's Molson stadium. There was a special magic in the air that night, but the young couple was sadly aware that all too soon the music would cease, and the spell would be broken. The memory of that last evening they would both treasure for the rest of their lives.

They had agreed a few days earlier that it would be best if Diana did not accompany Blake to the train station on the morning of his departure, so their final goodbyes were said in the taxi taking them home after the concert. Although they were both acutely conscious of their imminent parting, they tried to pretend this was no more than an ordinary date, and there would be many more to follow.

Blake gave her last-minute instructions about how to reach him in England. "And don't forget to number all your letters to me, and I'll do the same, that way we'll know if any are lost en route, and don't expect to hear from me for at least two or maybe three weeks. I have no idea when the convoy will leave, and for all I know we could be in Halifax for days," he told her, as he gave her a parting bear-hug, and whispered in her ear, "I'll always love you, Diana, always."

Her father picked Blake up early the following morning at the YMCA, where he had been staying during his leave, and

drove him to Windsor Station, a few blocks away. He helped him carry his gear into the concourse, which was awash with uniforms of every stripe: Army, Navy, Air Force, Red Cross, Salvation Army, even Boy Scouts and Girl Guides. It was a chaotic scene. There were young mothers clutching bulging suitcases, one with a pair of twins in harness and a baby strapped on her back. It seemed as if the whole world was on the move that morning, and there were long line-ups everywhere: at the luggage-checking counter, the coffee bar, the telephone kiosk, and the departure gate.

Roger stood chatting awkwardly with Blake in the line-up for a few minutes. Then, since he had an early meeting to attend, shook hands warmly with him, and patted his shoulder, wishing him good luck and a safe journey. At the last moment, on sudden impulse, he reached over and hugged him tightly for a few seconds before taking his leave. His eyes were moist as he made his way out of the station.

Instead of going directly to the office, he went home to make sure Diana was all right. By prior arrangement, he had allowed her to miss school that day. He found her exactly where he had left her, gazing forlornly out the sun-room window.

"I have to go to the office for a few hours, but why don't I pick you up about 11:30, and we'll have a nice lunch somewhere, and you can do a bit of shopping at Holt Renfrew's. I heard you say you needed a new raincoat a few days ago."

"I don't feel like shopping, thanks, Daddy, and I'm not in any mood to celebrate. I have such a dreadful ache in my chest where my heart used to be. I feel the sun may never shine on me again," she said in a sad little voice.

"Well then," said her father, trying to introduce a little levity into the conversation and perhaps see the glimmer of a smile on her face, "all the more reason to buy a new raincoat, wouldn't you say?" There was no reply to his attempt at humour.

The two weeks following Blake's departure seemed endless. Diana went to school as usual, but as soon as it was over for the day, she would rush home to see if the mail had arrived, and if there might be a letter from Blake. As the days dragged slowly by with no word from him, she became more and more despondent and more withdrawn. She had steeled herself not to expect a letter for at least two weeks, but once that deadline had passed, she sank deeper and deeper into a bottomless pit of depression. She ate almost nothing and seemed to be wasting away. Her sleep was fitful, and Roger could hear her moving restlessly around the house in the dead of night. He did his best to boost her spirits, and made various suggestions. "Why don't you invite a few of your friends, Peggy and Valerie and Jane, for lunch on Saturday, and I'll get tickets to the theatre?" All to no avail.

Exactly three weeks from the day of Blake's departure, on a morning when Diana had stayed home from school because she was not feeling well, the postman delivered a letter from overseas. It was addressed to Diana, and for a moment her heart leapt with joy at the thought that it was from Blake, but the sender's name was unfamiliar to her. It was from a Pilot Officer George Vickery, RCAF, c/o Canada House, London. Diana had a sudden terrifying premonition of disaster. Her heart was racing, beating a staccato tattoo against her ribs as she slit the envelope open with trembling fingers. It was dated June 15, 1943, and hand-written in a school-boyish scrawl.

> Dear Diana,
> You will not recognize my name, but Blake and I bunked together aboard ship, and became close friends during the voyage. We made a pact together that if something happened to either one of us en route, the other would notify a designated "very special person", who might otherwise not hear the news. I can't tell you how sorry I am to be the bearer of sad tidings,

but Blake was killed instantly in a freak accident on the very day we arrived here, which was yesterday. Because of censorship regulations, I cannot disclose details of what happened, but I was with him and I can tell you he died instantly, and that his last words and thoughts were of you. You were that "very special person" in his life.

With my deepest sympathy,
Yours faithfully,
George Vickery

Diana had no idea how long she sat there, shaking uncontrollably, staring blankly, dry-eyed, out the window, the letter lying in her lap. Afterwards, she had only a vague recollection of having felt chilled to the very marrow of her bones, as if the internal temperature of her body had dropped to zero. Her mind was a complete blank, as if she had undergone a surgical lobotomy. That was the state of profound shock in which Roger found her when he arrived home.

Roger was almost as devastated by the news of Blake's death as Diana had been, but his concern for his daughter's emotional state over-rode everything else. He called Lorna, told her briefly what had happened, and asked her to come. She would know, he told himself, how to comfort Diana, having been through this trauma herself when her own husband had been killed at Dunkirk, a few years earlier.

While waiting for Lorna, Roger persuaded Diana to lie down on the sofa, covered her with a heated blanket, filled two hot water bottles, and made her drink a cup of hot, strong, sweet tea. He sat with her in watchful silence until she finally dozed off out of sheer exhaustion. When she awoke, Lorna stroked her hand gently and said, "You have lost someone very

dear to you, Diana, and of course you are devastated. Grieving is a natural process, but it takes time. It goes through stages. As you know, I lost my husband, Jim, not long ago, so I know whereof I speak. We all cope with loss in our own way. Time is the only healer, and it seems to take forever. You'll find you won't notice any change from one week to the next, but suddenly when you look back a few months from now, you will realize how far you have progressed. So, take heart and take hope, dear. You'll get through this."

Diana's way of coping with her intense grief was to withdraw, turtle-like, into an inner shell. She was uncommunicative, despondent, and depressed. She did not call any of her friends, even to tell them about Blake's death. Several times, Roger heard her muffled sobs during the night.

Early one morning, about a week after the arrival of the letter, Roger was abruptly roused out of a deep sleep by a sound from down the hallway; a familiar sound, but one he had not heard in seventeen years. It was coming from Diana's bathroom. He was instantly wide-awake, on his feet, and down the hallway in a matter of seconds. He tapped on the door, "Diana, are you okay?" The gagging sound was repeated. His pulse was racing as he pushed the door open. Diana was bent over the washbasin, her face white as chalk. "Please God, no! Oh, no, Diana! Please tell me you're not pregnant!" The words were out of his mouth almost before he realized he had spoken aloud.

It took a few seconds for the shocking significance of what he had just witnessed to sink in, and his immediate reaction was more physical than cerebral. He felt as though he had been punched in the stomach with full force and had the wind knocked out of him. He felt disoriented, heartsick and stunned. His mind was almost unable to make sense of what had just happened.

"Oh, Daddy," Diana gasped weakly, gripping the edge of the counter to keep herself from falling. "I wish I were dead. What am I going to do?"

How he managed to pull himself together to respond, Roger did not know. He was in a profound state of shock, his mind reeling, but he heard himself say, "Right now you're going to get back into bed. I'll bring you some ginger ale and soda crackers. You'll feel better soon." Roger helped her into bed, put an extra blanket over her, and gently wiped her ashen face with a warm cloth. "You hold tight. I'll be back in a minute."

When he returned with the tray, Diana took a few sips of ginger ale, and a bite of one of the crackers, then lay back with her eyes closed. "Oh, Daddy, Daddy," she said tearfully, "I wish I were dead! I don't know if I can go on living."

Roger's heart ached for her. She was so young, so frail, and so vulnerable, but he said briskly, with an assurance he certainly did not feel, "Of course you can go on, and the way to do it is to put one foot in front of the other, every day of every week, and every month, until you reach your destination. I'm not saying it will be easy, but I'll be with you every step of the way. You got me through the worst year of my life, and I'm going to get you through this."

Later that day, when he had had time to think about it, he said, "I've been mulling the situation over in my mind for the last few hours, Diana, and I've come up with a plan.

"We're in a tight spot at the moment, but we're going to manoeuver our way out of it. We'll plan our strategy carefully and make all the right moves. Obviously, we can't remain in Montreal once your pregnancy becomes obvious. It so happens that our firm is building a huge new plant north of Barrie, Ontario. I can arrange a temporary transfer there to supervise the construction, and you will come with me. I'll get next year's syllabus from the principal of your school, and you can study at home while we're there, and when you go back to school in the spring, you won't have fallen behind your classmates.

"I have also been soul-searching, Diana. If anyone is to blame, it is I — not you, and not Blake. I should have been more vigilant. You were my responsibility, and it was my duty to protect you, but for some reason, I just didn't see this coming. I was blind-sided, caught off-guard, as it were. For your part, you were confronted with a situation you were totally unprepared to handle. You had no one to guide you. It is one thing to be mature physically, but emotional maturity is quite another thing. As the saying goes, one can't put an old head on young shoulders.

"The important thing, Diana, is that we keep this whole matter strictly to ourselves. You mustn't tell anyone about your pregnancy. That is essential if you are to have any kind of life afterwards. The one person I would like to discuss it with is Lorna, and I will only do that if you have no objection. She's a nurse, and I know she will be very supportive. Also, it is important that you keep in close touch, starting today, with your friends, Peggy, and Valerie and Jane and all the others. You are going to need them. Talk to them about Blake's death, and tell them I may have to go to Barrie for a few months in the fall, and that you will be going with me. We'll stay in Barrie until after the baby is born in February, and then we'll come back home, probably in early March. You'll go back to school, and graduate with your class in June."

"But, Daddy, we won't be able to keep it a secret once the baby is born," interrupted Diana. "If we come back to Montreal with a baby, everyone will know it is mine."

"We won't be bringing the baby to Montreal, Diana. I'll arrange the adoption, probably in Toronto, well in advance."

Diana stared at her father for a few seconds with an expression of shock on her face, as if unable to believe her ears. "I'm not going to give my baby away, Daddy! I thought you understood that! I won't. You can't ask me to do that," she said passionately.

"Diana," he replied gently, but firmly, "you have a decision to make in the next few days that will affect your whole life. It is probably the most important decision you will

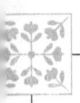

ever have to make. Everything hinges upon it—your future, as well as your baby's, so you must weigh the matter very carefully. I can't make this decision for you, but I've given the matter a great deal of thought these past few days, and I — "

"But, Daddy," Diana interrupted, sobbing, "You told me… just a few weeks ago that when I was born you were determined… never to give me up, or even put me in temporary foster care. You said you… would have fought the whole world to… keep me."

"And I would have," Roger replied, patiently, "but this is a very different situation. Your mother and I were married when you were born. There was no stigma to the birth. You are not a selfish person, Diana, but it would be both selfish and short-sighted of you to keep this baby. I know what I am talking about. Your baby is illegitimate. There would always be whispers, gossip, rumours, insinuations, innuendo. Your child would be emotionally scarred for life, and *your* life would be ruined. If you decide to do what is best for the baby, I will make certain he or she goes to a loving family, who has the means to give him—or her—the best possible chance in life. You owe that to Blake, as well as to yourself and your baby."

Diana wrestled with the problem for the next few days. Roger spent as much time with her as he could, realizing that, in addition to grieving for Blake, and the stress of pregnancy, she was at the same time undergoing a severe emotional crisis in having to make a decision about her baby's future. It was a heavy burden for a sixteen-year-old to shoulder, he thought to himself.

"I don't know what to do, Daddy," Diana said listlessly a few days later. "Everything just keeps going round and round in my head. It's as if I'm trying to find my way in the dark, but I don't know where I am, or where I'm going. I know you would never give me bad advice, so I will do whatever you think is best. I've talked to Lorna about it. She is very understanding, and agrees with you. I would really like it if she could come with us and stay while I'm waiting to have the baby."

Roger wrapped his arms around her, kissed the top of her head, and breathed a sigh of relief. "That's my girl!" he said. "You've made the right decision, dear. And Lorna suggested herself she could come and help us through this."

A visit to the doctor's office confirmed Diana's pregnancy, and an approximate due date of February 25th was given. Roger arranged his temporary transfer to Barrie—effective the first of September—and rented a furnished flat in an old schoolhouse, three miles north of Barrie, on the western shore of Lake Simcoe.

Diana's baby, a healthy little boy, was born a few days earlier than expected, on the nineteenth of February, in the Royal Victoria Hospital in Barrie. The birth was uneventful, and by prior arrangement with her doctor, the baby was whisked away by a nurse before Diana realized he had arrived. A few weeks later Diana, Roger and Lorna returned to Montreal. Diana had resolved to put the past year behind her, pick up the dropped stitches, and get on with her life. Roger breathed an immense sigh of relief that everything had gone according to plan.

Not long after Diana returned to Montreal, she received a handwritten letter, forwarded by a Toronto law firm. It gave her immense satisfaction, helped to assuage the lingering pain in her heart, and dissipate the doubts in her mind. The unsigned letter read as follows:

My Dear Benefactress,

You do not know me, and I do not, of course, have the slightest idea who you are, but my husband and I will be forever grateful to you for the immeasurable sacrifice you have made in giving up your son, and allowing us the joy of bringing him up as our own. I want to put your heart and mind at ease in assuring you that no baby was ever more lovingly welcomed into a family, or could be more dearly loved than he is. We lost our own little boy a year ago, and now, thanks to your magnificent generosity, it seems he has miraculously been restored to us. Blessings be upon you and yours for all time.

Act Two: Montreal, April 1944

Diana poured her father a cup of coffee, and sat down opposite him at the kitchen table. "It doesn't seem possible we've been away from Montreal for six months, does it, Dad?" (When, Roger wondered to himself, had she started calling him *Dad*?) "Six months is a huge chunk out of my life, and yet, now that we're back here, it seems as if I've never been away at all. So much has happened, but it's almost as though this past year has been a dream. I feel I sleep-walked through that time and the whole sequence of events; falling in love with Blake, losing him, finding out I was pregnant, moving to Barrie, having a baby, and giving him up for adoption. In a way, it's as if all this happened to someone else, and I've only heard about it second-hand."

"Perhaps that's nature's way of blotting out some of the harshness of reality," said Roger thoughtfully. "I'm so proud of the way you've handled all this, Diana. No one gets through life without sadness and sorrow, but you've had more than your share of it this past year."

"I only got through it by following the advice you and Lorna gave me, Dad, by taking one day at a time, and putting one foot in front of another every day, every week, and every month until I got where I had to go. This has been a learning and life-changing experience for me. I had to grow up quickly, and find out about life the hard way. I know it has changed me, and altered my perception of who I am. I read somewhere recently that in Spanish and Portuguese colonies, slaves were given something called 'The Right of Self-Purchase.' If they could pay the required price, they could buy their own freedom. I feel I've done that, and now I'm determined to put this past year behind me, and move ahead with my life. Thank you for getting me through it all, Dad—you and Lorna. I couldn't have done it without the two of you."

"Nor could I have survived without you, all those years ago," replied Roger. "You've evened the score, that's all."

Diana's return to school following the Easter holidays

was uneventful. Her friends welcomed her back without seeming to notice anything different about her, but in fact it was not the old Diana who returned. There was a new maturity about her, a new sense of purpose, slowly taking root. Roger noticed the difference at once. "Diana has grown up these past few months," he told Lorna. "She tells me she's determined to put this past year behind her, as if it had never happened, and move ahead with her life."

The diligence Diana had shown in applying herself to her studies while she was away paid off. She sailed through the spring exams, and was rewarded by receiving early admission acceptance to McGill University. When Roger congratulated her, she replied, "You know, Dad, all my life, until recently, I coasted through school. I never felt challenged, so I never put any effort into achieving anything. As long as I passed, I was satisfied. I'm much more motivated now. I'm going to work hard, and I've made up my mind I'm not going to get emotionally involved with anyone."

"That's probably wise," said Roger, "but all work and no play isn't a good idea, either. You have to find the right balance—so don't cut yourself off. By the way, changing the subject, I hear that our friend Robbie joined the Navy while we were away. He's been a Sea Cadet since he was twelve, and he couldn't wait to be old enough to enlist. I must get his address from his father and send him a note."

"Be sure to say hello from me when you write," said Diana. "I haven't seen much of him these last few years, since he went to boarding school, but you know he was my first friend on the street when we moved here to Strathcona Avenue. I was in kindergarten, and I remember he rescued me from some big kids who were throwing snowballs at me. He told me to let him know if anyone ever bothered me again, and said he'd beat them up."

"He was always your champion, wasn't he?" said her father, smiling.

The Second World War, which had ravaged Europe

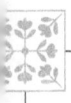

for nearly six years, raged on. May 1945 finally—and quite suddenly—brought victory in Europe for the Allied Forces, but the fighting in the Far East against the Japanese was far from over. The troops who had fought so valiantly to defeat Hitler would not be returning home to their wives and children, but would instead be going to the Pacific arena to fight the Japanese. The mood in Canada that summer was somber. One powerful enemy had been defeated, but the feeling was that the conflict with Japan would continue for the foreseeable future.

Suddenly, early in August 1945, the war ended; not with a whimper, but with a very loud bang. On August 6, the American Air Force dropped the first-ever atomic bomb on the city of Hiroshima, and when the Japanese did not immediately surrender, a second bomb was dropped on Nagasaki. Finally the Second World War, after six long, weary years, had come to an abrupt end.

This was the state of world affairs when Diana started at McGill University in September of 1945. Hundreds of battle-seasoned veterans were either returning to university, or enrolling for the first time. There were many more male students than there were female, and Diana was soon caught up in the social whirl of campus life. She was not short of either admirers or invitations. She attended a few fraternity parties, and dances at the student union, but Roger was troubled to see her heart wasn't in it.

She began refusing invitations to dances and parties. When Roger asked her why, she replied, "Most of them are so boring, Dad, even the veterans who think they're such sophisticated men of the world. They're only interested in having a good time. The only book some of them are familiar with is Winnie the Pooh, and that's because their mothers read it to them in kindergarten. I'd much rather stay home by myself than go out and be bored stiff. Oh, by the way, guess who I ran into in the library today? Robbie! He just got his discharge from the Navy, and he's in first-year science. He drove me

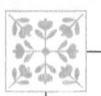

home after class in his new car, and said he'd drop over tonight to say hello to you."

"Great!" Roger replied. "I'll be glad to see him again, and hear how he can afford to buy a car, especially a new one."

"He told me his grandfather had set up a trust fund for his education years ago, and now a big fat cheque is deposited in his bank account every month."

"Nice work, if you can get it," commented Roger.

A few days before Christmas, sitting in front of the fireplace after dinner, Diana, who had been very quiet all evening, suddenly said, "A lot of the vets at McGill are getting married. What would your reaction be, Dad, if I told you Robbie has asked me to marry him?"

"I'd be very surprised," he said. "Are you serious?" She nodded in assent.

"Do you love him?"

She hesitated for a moment before replying. "I don't really know, Dad. I think so. I think I've always loved Robbie, although not in the way I loved Blake. That could only happen once in anyone's lifetime. What I do know for certain, though, is that I like Robbie a whole lot more than any of the other boys I know."

"Does he love you?" asked Roger.

Again she nodded her head. "Yes, I think so. In fact, I'm sure he does."

"I'd say that's a pretty good start for a marriage, Diana, better than most probably. Will you tell him about Blake and the baby?"

"Oh, I already told him weeks ago, Dad. I wouldn't have thought of *not* telling him."

"What was his reaction?" Roger asked.

"All he said was that he was sorry, and he wished he had known at the time, because he might have been able to help. He hasn't mentioned it since."

There was silence between them for a moment or two, and then Roger said, "What would you say if I told you Lorna

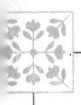

and I have been talking about getting married?"

"I'd say, Hallelujah! What took you so long?" she exclaimed excitedly, jumping up from her chair and throwing her arms around her father. "Why don't we make it a double wedding? We could give each other away."

Act Three: Montreal 1965

"I'm so glad you and Lorna are back from Bermuda, Grampa," said Alison, as she poured her grandfather a cup of tea. "There's something Ainsley and I need to talk to you about. We didn't want to worry you while you were on holiday, but Mom's been acting really weird this past month. Dad's death was a terrible shock to her, and to all of us, of course, but it's been nearly a year since then, and we thought she was pretty much back to normal. At the time, she seemed to handle the situation so much better than we would ever have thought. She was fine at Christmas, don't you think, Ainsley?" she said, turning to her twin sister, who was perched on a loveseat beside their grandfather. "Neither of us noticed anything unusual until a few weeks ago, when she got a letter from England that she acted very mysterious about. A few days later, she suddenly announced at dinner that she needed to get away for a while. The next thing we knew, she'd booked a flight to England, and left the very next day."

"Who did she go with?" asked Roger.

"As far as we know," said Ainsley, "she went alone, and she's never before gone anywhere in her whole life by herself. She was very evasive about her plans, and that's not like her. She's always been so open about everything, and now she's become downright secretive. Do you think it could be a delayed reaction to Dad's death, Grampa?"

"Hard to say," replied Roger, looking thoughtful. "Do you know where to reach her in case of emergency, or when she is expected to be back?"

"No," answered Alison. "She's been gone nearly two weeks, and we haven't heard a peep. We keep hoping every day there'll be a letter or a cable from her. The thing is,

Grampa, we don't want to worry you, but we just don't know what to do."

"I'll call her travel agent first thing in the morning. He can probably tell us when she is due to return," said their grandfather as he rose to leave. "In the meantime, don't worry, girls. No news is generally good news."

Roger telephoned his granddaughters the following morning to report that the travel agency had not booked a return flight for Diana. A few days later, a letter arrived from Diana, post-marked London. It read as follows:

> Dear Alison and Ainsley,
>
> I've decided to spend a few more days in London before returning home. I am having such a good time; I don't want to leave. Who knew swinging London could be so much fun? I almost feel young again. I've been taken to the theatre several times, and yesterday I bought a lovely new tweed suit at Harrods which I plan to wear to a special lunch at the Savoy Hotel later today. I hope all is well on the home front. Love to you both, and to Lorna and Dad, if they're back from Bermuda.
>
> See you soon,   Mummy

"What do you make of that, Grampa?" said Alison, who had just read the letter to him over the telephone.

"Well, it's a relief to know where she is, and that she's all right," he replied, "but the letter doesn't sound at all like her, does it?"

"No, she's positively euphoric. You don't suppose she's smoking pot, or sniffing glue, do you?"

"Surely not," said her grandfather, shocked at the very thought, "but something is going on with her. I just can't think what. I wish I knew."

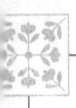

"Hang on, Grampa," said Alison. "Ainsley wants to say something to you."

"Hi, Grampa. This is Ainsley. I just had a thought. Do you suppose she's met some gigolo, or some con artist who's after her money? She's lived such a sheltered existence all her life—I don't think she has any idea what goes on in the world. Wouldn't it be awful if someone like that talked her into getting married?"

A few days later Diana returned home, rejuvenated, it seemed, in mind, body and spirit. She had a new chic hair-do, and several smart new outfits, with the new mini hemline, so fashionable in London, but which shocked her daughters, as the style had not yet crossed the Atlantic. Almost at once, the twins noticed she began receiving long-distance telephone calls, with charges reversed, at strange hours of the day and night, as well as a steady stream of letters from England, which she read in private. A few weeks after her return, she made another trip back to London, and while she was away, the letters and telephone calls ceased, indicating she was visiting the writer of the letters. Roger and the twins were concerned.

It was during Diana's second trip back to England that Roger happened to run into her bank manager, whom he had known for many years. "Roger," he said, taking him aside, "I've been meaning to call you about this. Remember, I haven't said a word to you, but somebody ought to be keeping an eye on Diana's financial affairs these days, if you take my meaning? A word to the wise, and all that, you know."

A few days later Roger received a cryptic telephone call from his lawyer, who was also an old friend, hinting, without actually saying so, that Diana was planning to make changes to her will. Roger had been reluctant to get involved in Diana's financial affairs, but this tip-off from his lawyer was a clarion call to action. He felt duty bound to protect not only his daughter, but his granddaughters as well, from anyone who might be out to defraud them. He tried to quiz Diana as tactfully as he could when she returned from England, but she was immediately on the defensive, and abruptly changed the subject. The twins reported to him that the letters and collect telephone calls had resumed again, and Diana's strange behaviour continued as before.

Sitting at the dining room table after dinner one evening, shortly after her return, surrounded by the twins, Lorna and her father, Diana suddenly said, "While I have you all here together, I have something important I want to say to you. It's this. During my visit to England a few months ago, I met a man who has become inexpressibly dear to me, and utterly indispensable to my future happiness. I know this will come as a shock to all of you, but I hope you will be able to accept this new relationship in my life without being judgmental. I have invited him to come to Montreal for an extended visit, so you can all get to know him. His plane will be arriving at 2:40 tomorrow afternoon. I'll meet him at the airport and bring him back here. I hope, for my sake, you will all do everything you can to make him feel welcome in our midst."

There was a moment of stunned silence in the room. Roger was the first to find his voice. "Frankly, Diana, I have to say I think it was very unwise of you to invite someone you scarcely know to stay here in your house, particularly when you have two teenage daughters. He might be an axe murderer or a pervert, for all you know. Put him up in a hotel downtown if you must, but don't have him here under your roof. That's my advice, for what it's worth. I'm sorry to be so blunt, but that's how I feel." He pushed his chair back slightly from the table, crossed his legs, and folded his arms resolutely across his chest. Diana could see he was ready to do battle.

"Well, knowing how protective you've always been towards me," she replied as calmly as she could, "I was fully expecting this kind of over-reaction from you, Dad. I appreciate your concern for me, but I have invited him to stay here, and I'm not going back on my invitation. I don't wish to discuss the matter further."

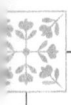

Turning to her step-mother, she said pleasantly, "He'll be here for dinner tomorrow evening, Lorna. I hope you and Dad will join us."

Shortly after lunch the following day, Alison telephoned her grandfather. "Grampa," she said, "We've got a problem! Mom just called. She was on her way to the airport, and she's been involved in a minor traffic accident... No. No, nobody was injured, but she's in a real flap. She can't leave the scene of the accident till the police arrive, and she wants us to meet the plane, so Ainsley and I are—"

"I'll drive you there," interrupted Roger. "Lorna and I will pick you up in five minutes."

There was very little traffic on the road, and Roger made good time driving to Dorval Airport. Secretly, he was delighted at this unexpected turn of events. It would give him a chance to size the fellow up, and take whatever action was required to get rid of him. The twins chatted excitely in the back seat.

"By the way, does anyone know this man's name?" asked Lorna.

"Yes, I do," said Alison. "Mom just told me today. His name is Keith Wilkie, but we haven't any idea what he looks like, and he won't know us. I think we'll have to have him paged. What'll we say, Grampa? How about something like, 'Will con artist Keith Wilkie, arriving from London, please come to the information desk and identify himself?' Or maybe we could just tell Mom he wasn't on the plane. What do you think he'll look like, Ainsley?"

"I think he'll be one of those aging Lotharios who prey on unsuspecting, lonely, well-heeled widows. Anyway, I'm not looking forward to meeting this character and having to make nice with him."

"Stop worrying about it," said Roger, through gritted teeth, "I'll handle this fellow. Just leave him to me. He has no idea what he's up against. I suppose your mother paid for his flight here, but if he thinks he's going to get his hands on any more of her money, he's in for a nasty shock. If he's smart, he'll get on the next plane out of here and go right back where he came from; that is, if he has the wherewithal to buy himself a ticket. You know, girls, the thing that surprises me most about this whole business is that your mother didn't have more common sense than to get mixed up with someone like this. It's not like her to be taken in."

"Roger, it's not really fair to prejudge him," protested Lorna, always the peace-maker. "We should give him the benefit of the doubt, at least until we meet him."

"What I'll give him will be the benefit of the boot," said Roger truculently, literally spoiling for a fight with this unwelcome interloper.

On reaching the main terminal building, they went directly to the Arrivals area. It was crowded with people, standing in little clumps behind the barrier, all craning their necks to identify a familiar face amongst the passengers streaming through the gate.

"Grampa," said Alison, "would you like me to have him paged? Otherwise, we'll never find him when we have no idea what he looks like."

Before her grandfather could reply, an elderly lady standing next to them spoke up, "Excuse me, I couldn't help overhearing. Are you by any chance here to meet a passenger from London? I sat beside a nice young man on the plane, such a nice man he was, and very excited—but nervous to be meeting his new family. He hopes so much you will like and accept him. So there's no need to have him paged, because you'll have no trouble at all recognizing him!"

"But what do you mean? Why do you think he is the one we are meeting?" Roger asked.

"He's the image of you, sir, just a newer model, that's all. You must be the grandfather he's never met."

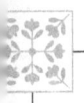

The Sinking of the City of Benares

I have long since forgotten the name of the woman, but I have never forgotten the story she told. She was entirely unremarkable, even nondescript to look at—a middle-aged woman who had had a career teaching in Liverpool prior to the Second World War.

I met her at the house of a friend, where she was staying as a guest, and I happened to sit next to her at tea. The events she recounted were in sharp contrast to her insignificant appearance. "Adventure" was not a word one would have associated with her in any way. She looked like what she was— a person who had always been on the sidelines of life, a most unlikely candidate for a major role in a wartime disaster—but what a story she recounted.

To make conversation, I asked if this visit was the first journey she had made to Canada, to which she replied, "Well actually I set out once before, but unfortunately I didn't make it that time." When I asked what had happened to interfere with her plans, I certainly didn't expect the response she gave.

"I had been teaching at an elementary school in Liverpool for several years in the late 1930s." She continued, "After the war began, I responded to an advertisement from the Children's Overseas Reception Board to accompany a group of children being evacuated from Liverpool to safety in North America.

"I was offered the job, and accepted readily, as I had no family responsibilities at that time and loved working with children. The post offered me the chance to see something of the world, while also contributing a little to the war effort. I was assigned to the ship *The City of Benares*, carrying over 400 passengers and crew, including nearly 100 children.

"We set sail from Liverpool on September 13, 1940. A few days later, on the evening of September seventeenth, a few hundred miles off the coast of Ireland, our ship was torpedoed by a German U-boat. The torpedo struck the ship just below the water line. Some of the children were killed in the explosion, some were trapped in their cabins, and some, as young as five years of age, ended up on deck in their dressing gowns, still clutching their teddy bears. We huddled together on deck while we waited for the crew to make ready the lifeboats. The first of these was filled with children, their guardians and a member of the crew. As the lifeboat was being lowered, it struck the side of the ship and the occupants were all pitched into the sea. We watched in horror as people struggled against the massive waves, but nothing could be done to save them.

"Our group was next, and the children gathered round me, shrieking in terror as we were seated in the second lifeboat and lowered into the sea. We made it safely, although with a good deal of water in the boat, but there I was, with my group of terrified children and a lascar seaman."

At this point, I had to interrupt the narrative, as I didn't know what a lascar was. My informant had to explain that this was a term used to describe a sailor from the Indian subcontinent. Lascars were subject to a special type of contract and were almost always poorly paid. Apart from this one interruption, I listened with horrified fascination to her story. So vivid was her description that I almost felt as if I were there, with her and the petrified children in the icy ocean waters.

She continued, "We were adrift for over a week, and food and water were scarce. The lascar carefully rationed out the small amounts of each that we had. I remember one day we shared a single peach between us, each getting one tiny portion. Conditions were dreadful on the lifeboat, and at least one child died each day. During the night, the lascar and I would surreptitiously tip their bodies overboard.

"On the eighth day relief came, and we were rescued by a passing destroyer. The children and I and the lascar were winched aboard. An officer helped to wrap us all in dry blankets, and then escorted us into the warmth of the ship, where we were seen at once by the ship's doctor and then given food and drink. The officer then graciously offered me the use of his cabin for

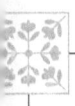

the night. I slept soundly that night for the first time in eight days. It was in conversation with other crew members later that I learned that the gallant officer who had surrendered his cabin to me was none other than Lieutenant Mountbatten — Prince Philip, the future husband of the Queen!"

I listened with rapt attention to her story. Of course, I believed every word she had told me… and did so for the next sixty years. It was only quite recently that I heard on the radio that it had been an anniversary of the sinking of *The City of Benares*, and my daughter had watched a dramatization on television about it. When she mentioned this to me, I told her the story I had heard. She was fascinated and turned to her computer to find more details. Imagine my surprise when she told me that from the whole ship, one lifeboat only had been rescued. This had been occupied by Mary Cornish, an English music teacher who, with a group of children, had survived in the lifeboat for over a week. Of the lascar, there was no mention. I was astounded to realize that the whole story which I had been told and which so captured my imagination was quite false. The presence of Prince Philip in particular was a pure fantasy on her part. Naval records show that at the time he was far from the North Atlantic.

I am a trusting person, and I can't understand why anyone should invent such a story about herself. Was it simply that my storyteller, this non-descript little woman, craved attention so much that she had felt driven to adopt the dramatic story of Mary Cornish and present herself to the world in the starring role? The more I think about her, the more my original outrage at being duped turns to pity. It must have been that her life was so drab and colourless that she had taken and embellished the story for her own purposes. She had doubtless dined out on this fiction many times over the years.

Adrienne Rich once said "Every journey into the past is complicated by delusions, false memories, false naming of real events."

Perhaps we should not judge her too harshly.

An Officer and a Gentleman

rsula spotted the young Royal Air Force officer the moment he walked into the canteen, where she was on duty as a volunteer hostess that morning in July 1943. The whole world, it seemed, was engaged in a titanic struggle, a life-and-death battle between the forces of good and evil, but this fact was of little or no interest to Ursula Sloane. She had more important matters on her mind: namely herself and her own small world.

Ursula was in her mid-fifties, as vain as a peacock about her appearance, and very class-conscious. She was as thin as a wraith, almost to the point of emaciation, reminiscent of Wallis Warfield Simpson, she of the abdication kerfuffle in 1936. Like Wallis, Ursula believed that a woman could never be too rich or too thin. She enjoyed playing the role of châtelaine of the canteen. She was coyly flirtatious with the young officers who frequented the facility. The other ranks she served with icy politeness.

She glanced again, admiringly, at the RAF officer. "What a handsome young man he is," Ursula thought to herself. "He reminds me of Tyrone Power. I don't think he's been in here before. I would certainly remember him."

Noting his rank from the configuration of the bars on his sleeve, and impressed by the ribbons on his chest, she approached the young man, smiled warmly, and said, "Good morning, Squadron Leader. May I get you a cup of coffee?"

"Actually, I'd prefer a cup of tea, if you don't mind," he replied in a crisp upper-class English accent. Ursula hurried away, brought back the tea and seated herself beside him. Leaning towards him slightly, she rested one elbow on her knee, chin cupped in the palm of her hand. She always felt that was one of her most attractive poses.

"How do you like Canada?" she enquired.

"I've only just arrived madam, but, please, may I introduce myself? My name is Clive Somerset. May I ask your name?"

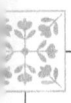

"Of course; I'm Mrs. Victor Sloane. My friends call me Ursula."

"Then I shall call you Ursula, if I may. I'm sure we shall become friends. I can tell by your manner that you are, as we say at home, one of 'us'."

"How perceptive of you." Ursula replied. "My husband is very prominent in the business community in this country. My son is an officer in the Navy and my daughter is engaged in important war work in Ottawa."

"But you're far too young to have children old enough to serve in the war," Clive protested.

"Thank you, kind sir," she replied, beaming at him and batting her eyelashes.

He then proceeded to tell her a little bit about himself, elaborating on his career and his many sorties in the Battle of Britain. Ursula was captivated by Clive's good looks and charm, and she decided to invite him home for dinner that evening, thinking he would be a good catch for her daughter. Ursula explained that her husband would not be at home that evening. "He often works late, because he's one of those "dollar-a-year" men who advise the Prime Minister from time to time." Clive was very interested and asked questions about what her husband was doing. "It's all very hush-hush," she said. "I wouldn't even have mentioned that much except I know you are an officer and a gentleman."

Later that evening, she told her husband Victor all about this enchanting young officer. "He's just what I always wanted in a son-in-law. We shall have to cultivate him. He's here on a special assignment for British intelligence, working undercover."

The next evening, at Ursula's invitation, Clive returned to the house to meet Victor, who was immediately suspicious of him. Later that evening, he said to Ursula, "From what I know of counterintelligence, they would not pick someone like Clive. They recruit inconspicuous types who blend in with the landscape. In any case, he should not be telling you that he is on a secret mission. There's something phoney about him. I don't trust him."

"But he's a decorated war hero," protested Ursula. "I'm sure he's genuine. I trust him completely."

Victor said nothing more about the matter to his wife, but the next day he reported what Ursula had told him to the intelligence services.

Clive continued to make daily visits to the canteen, turning on the charm for Ursula. It came as a complete shock to her when, a few days later, two Mounties arrived at the canteen. They briefly interrogated Clive, pulled him to his feet, handcuffed him and frog-marched him out and into a waiting staff car.

Ursula couldn't wait to tell Victor about the incident when he got home that evening. "It was most extraordinary. Clive has been arrested. The police told me he has been impersonating an officer. I can't believe it. I protested and tried to intervene, but they wouldn't listen to me."

Victor smiled. "Well, I can believe it. I was informed about his arrest. This young man completely pulled the wool over your eyes. He was not a Squadron Leader in the RAF, nor was he decorated. In fact, he is not a member of any of the armed services. He is, however, in deep trouble. Impersonating an officer is an extremely serious offence. Not only that, but the authorities suspect that he may be the enemy agent who they know came ashore in the Gulf of St. Lawrence from a German U-boat a week or so ago."

"I hope you've learned a lesson about not taking people at face value, Ursula." He was tempted to add, "I told you so," but wisely refrained, knowing from long experience that Ursula did not take kindly to such remarks.

Ursula frowned in silence for a few minutes, then her face brightened up. "There was a most distinguished-looking young naval officer at the canteen this morning. I think he might be a good catch for Amy."

Victor rolled his eyes and excused himself to work in his study.

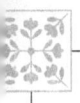

Closing the Circle

I would have thought one could safely say, without fear of contradiction, that the word "romance" does not immediately spring to mind in connection with a senior citizens' residence. But, as it turned out, I would have been wrong. Romance, as I was to discover, was not only alive and well, but actually flourishing, at the Golden Gates Retirement Centre.

The reason I happened to be at the Centre that day was because I had offered to investigate it for an elderly friend who was no longer able to live on her own.

The moment I stepped over the threshold, I was aware that something unusual was going on. The newel post of the wide, impressive, curving staircase was decorated with a large white satin bow and the adjoining lounge was clearly decked-out for a formal occasion.

"This has all the earmarks of a wedding," I said to a woman of about my own age who was arranging a bowl of flowers on the grand piano. "Yes, indeed. There is a wedding taking place here today, a very special wedding," she replied with a wide smile, "and I am the daughter of the bride. Are you here to visit one of the residents?"

"No, I am here on a tour of inspection for an elderly friend. Perhaps I should come back another day."

"Oh, do stay for the wedding now that you're here," said the daughter of the bride, introducing herself as Elaine Roberts. "The wedding will take place in less than an hour, and if you like, I can give you a brief history of how all this came about. It really is a most interesting story."

"I'd love to hear it," I replied. We found two comfortable chairs and settled ourselves.

"I'll have to take you back a few years in time," Elaine began, "otherwise you won't understand why this wedding is so romantic. Today's bride, my mother, whose name then was Louise Leduc, was born in Quebec City in 1918, shortly before the end of the First World War. When my mother turned eighteen and had completed her education, she was invited to spend the winter social season with her favourite aunt in Montreal. This was the most exciting thing that had ever happened to her. After living in parochial Quebec City all her life, the hustle and bustle of cosmopolitan Montreal was intoxicating for the naïve teenager. She loved everything about it, the sophistication, the Anglo culture, which of course she had never experienced, and the glittering social life of the city.

"What made it all the more exciting for her was that at the very first ball she ever attended, which happened to be the annual ball of the St. Andrew's Society, she met a young farmer from Alberta, by the name of Angus Cameron. He was handsome, he was witty, he was charming, and the two of them fell madly in love with each other at first sight."

Elaine explained that the reason Angus happened to be in Montreal that particular winter was because his father, a cattle-breeder, had ordered some prize livestock from Scotland, and had sent his son to take delivery of the shipment in Montreal, and to escort the animals to Alberta by freight train. Unfortunately, or perhaps in some respects, fortunately, winter came early that year. The St. Lawrence River was frozen solid by the end of November, and would not be navigable again for several months. Delivery of the animals could not take place until the following spring.

Since there was very little work to be done on the farm during the winter months, Angus suggested to his father that he remain where he was until the shipment arrived in Montreal in early spring. This, of course, suited young Angus down to the ground.

"During that winter," she continued, "since they were both "on holiday," they spent every day together. They were completely in love. They wanted to become engaged and plan a wedding, but Louise's father would not hear of it. "You are far too young, and you scarcely know each other, but if you still feel the same in a year's time, I will think again."

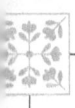

In the spring, when the ice melted on the St. Lawrence, the cattle arrived from Scotland. Angus had to return home to Alberta, but the two wrote to each other almost every day, pledging their love.

All this happened just prior to the outbreak of war in September 1939. Responding to the mood of the time, Angus enlisted in the Royal Canadian Air Force and began training as a pilot. When this was completed, he was immediately posted overseas. Before flying out to England, he was able to visit Louise in Quebec City. Their reunion was short, but their love proved as strong as ever. They promised each other that they would marry after the war.

For the first few weeks, Angus and Louise wrote to each other nearly every day. However, on his first mission, Angus' plane was shot down over the Dutch coast. All the crew was killed in the crash, but Angus' body was never recovered. In published casualty lists, he was reported as missing in action. Louise clung to the hope that somehow he had survived. Eventually that hope was crushed; Angus was officially declared presumed dead. Louise was distraught. She would neither eat nor sleep; she wanted just to die. Months passed, and her agony very gradually began to lessen. Eventually, Louise came to accept that she would never see Angus again. Life slowly began to resume a more normal pattern. She took a job as an interpreter, moved into a new apartment, made new friends and even went to the odd party. At one of these, she heard of an old friend who had been badly wounded in the war and desperately needed help to enable him to rebuild his life. Partly out of pity, partly out of a wish to make a contribution to the war effort, and partly in memory of Angus, she decided to help, and moved into an apartment near him. With her free time, she was able to look after him and help with his physiotherapy. Months passed and he gradually recovered his strength. At the same time, their relationship started to change; no longer nurse and patient, they became close friends. More so, in fact; he had fallen in love with her and wanted to marry her. For her part, she felt great affection for him, but not love. However, realizing that she had to put the past behind her and get on with her life, she assumed a brave face and married him.

"He, of course, was my father," Elaine explained. "Despite this rather inauspicious start, they had a long and happy life together in Montreal. My father died in his late sixties, and was greatly mourned by his wife and family. Left quite alone, my mother moved into this retirement centre.

"Now I have to tell you what happened to Angus," Elaine continued. "As I told you, the crew had all been killed in the crash, but miraculously, Angus survived. A Dutch resistance fighter, who found him unconscious and badly wounded, had rescued him from the wreckage. The fighter's son had been killed in the war, so he and his wife hid Angus, and nursed him back to health. After many months, Angus had sufficiently recovered and was desperate to escape from Holland and rejoin his squadron in England. As he tried to make his way back to the Dutch coast, unable to speak either Dutch or German and possessing only forged papers, he was caught by the Germans at a checkpoint, after which he was sent to a prisoner of war camp in Germany. There he stayed, until liberated at the end of the war.

"During his time in the prison camp, what kept him alive and fed his spirits was the thought of Louise. Through the Red Cross he tried to contact her to let her know he was still alive; his letters received no answer. We know now that it was probably by this time that Louise had moved away from Quebec City and had changed her name after marrying. She certainly never received his letters.

"When the war ended, Angus was eventually repatriated and returned to Canada. His boat from Europe arrived at Halifax and he was put on a train back to Alberta. He passed much of the long journey dreaming of the happy times he had spent with Louise in Montreal. He was jolted from his reverie when his eye was caught by a picture in a

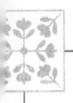

newspaper someone had left on the train. There was something familiar about the woman. The caption to the picture read 'Mr. and Mrs. David Armstrong at the Victory Ball,' and it continued, 'Mrs. Armstrong, the daughter of the late Captain James LeDuc of Quebec City, has recently moved to Montreal and lives in Westmount.'"

"As you can imagine," Elaine continued, "Angus stared at the picture in disbelief, but it really was his Louise. She had betrayed him. They had promised to be true to each other no matter what, and she had done this to him. Had she received his letters and been too ashamed to reply, or did she think that he was dead? What should he do?

"Throughout the long journey to Alberta, he agonized over the situation. Should he find Mrs. Armstrong and confront her? What would she do? Would she leave her husband for him? And if she did, could she and Angus ever be happy with the guilt of a marriage breakup hanging over them? In the end, he decided that the decent thing was to accept the situation and leave well enough alone.

"When he got back to Alberta, he began to rebuild his life. He used his money from the Re-Establishment Credits to qualify as an accountant. He set up a business in his hometown and over time, the business prospered. Later still, he married a local girl, had two children and lived a happy life, until his wife's death at the age of seventy. At that point, one of his daughters, who had moved to Montreal, suggested that he retire there to be closer to her. After a few years of happy retirement, he reluctantly uprooted himself again and moved into this retirement centre, not far from where his daughter lived.

"In the dining-room at the centre that first evening, he happened to notice a woman sitting at a nearby table. Something about her was familiar—the way she moved her head, the way she gestured with her hands. His heart beat frantically; he could scarcely breathe. Could it be, was it possible that this was Louise?

"The woman finished her dinner and left the table. In a daze Angus followed to find the woman taking coffee in the lounge. With his heart pounding, he approached her. "By some miracle," he stammered, "are you, were you, Louise LeDuc?" The woman turned pale. "Angus?" she gasped, "I...I...I thought you were dead!" She burst into tears, but they were tears of joy. From that moment on, they seemed to recapture the careless joy of their first love. They have truly been granted a second chance to make their lives together. So there you have it: that is the story of how my mother was reunited with the love of her life."

"What a romantic story!" I replied." I'm so glad I happened to come here today. I wouldn't have missed this for anything."

Elaine looked at her watch. "The ceremony will be starting soon, and I am playing *The Wedding March* on the piano. How would it be if I found you a seat in the front row, so you'll have a good view of the whole proceedings?"

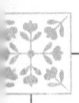

Once Bitten…

Phyllis put down the letter she had just received and gazed at the framed wedding photograph that had always graced her mantelpiece. The bride, Alice, was beautifully dressed in a full-length white satin gown, and was surrounded by Phyllis, the maid of honour, and five formally-clad bridesmaids. At the bride's side stood the handsome groom, George, and behind him his best man and five ushers. It had been the wedding of year in Red Deer, Alberta in 1938. The radiant happiness of the bride and groom portrayed no hint of the tragedy that would befall them when both Alice and her baby died in childbirth before the year was out.

Gazing at the photograph, Phyllis reflected on all the events that had happened in her life since then. She remembered how she had tried to be a comfort to George, and her gradual realization that her feelings for him and his for her had blossomed into love. By the time war was declared and George had enlisted in the Navy, there was an unspoken understanding between them that after the war, they would make a life together.

George wrote frequently from various ports around the world where his ship took him, and his letters were filled with references to his plans for their future together. Phyllis, hoping that their paths might cross, enlisted in the Navy herself, and was sent to Halifax, where she spent the war years.

George's letters gradually became less frequent, and early in 1942, his letters ceased altogether for several weeks. Phyllis was concerned that something might have happened to him, but when she finally did hear from him again, it was a blow that she did not expect. Even after all these years, she remembered how her heart stopped when she read the words that were now engraved in her memory. "As you know, I have been billeted with a family here in Scotland for the last two months, while my ship was being repaired. They have been so kind to me. They treat me like their son who went missing in action a year ago. I have become involved with their daughter, Bonnie, and felt I was honour-bound to marry her when I learned she was pregnant with my child. I hope you can find it in your heart to forgive me. I wish you well, always." Her world had come crashing down around her.

Phyllis busied herself with her duties in the Navy and when the war finally came to an end, she made a new life for herself in Ottawa in the civil service. She had an active social life, but never had a serious relationship with any of the men she met. Her heart, it seemed, belonged to George.

After several years, out of the blue, she received a letter from George, saying that he was coming to Ottawa on business and suggesting that they might meet for lunch. Although thrilled to hear from him, Phyllis thought long and hard before accepting the invitation. She was reluctant to open an old wound, but her curiosity and her affection for him won out. During the lunch, George looked across the table at her and, taking her hand in his, said wistfully, "I wish I'd had the good sense to marry you all those years ago."

That was the beginning of the intimate relationship that developed between them.

Over the next few years, he arranged to come frequently to Ottawa on business and always managed to find time for her, but explained that he could not leave his wife, as she was now an invalid and dependent on him. Against her better judgment, Phyllis convinced herself that their relationship was not hurting anyone, and George would one day be free. However, as it continued year after year, doubts began to creep into her mind. He seemed evasive about his wife's condition, but still Phyllis clung to the hope that he would eventually be able to marry her.

The day finally came when George announced his wife's death, but he told Phyllis that although he would still continue to see her in Ottawa, it would be inappropriate for him to remarry so quickly. She reluctantly agreed, ignoring the

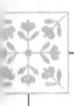

little warning signals that were flashing through her subconscious mind.

Phyllis's misgivings about George were fully vindicated when, on the twenty-fifth anniversary of Alice and George's marriage, she received an unexpected letter from her old friend, Penny, still living in Red Deer. Penny wrote that although they had not been in touch for a long time, she had thought of Phyllis as the anniversary approached, as they had both been in the bridal party, and knew she would be interested to hear the local gossip.

Penny's letter continued, "You perhaps remember Dora Jones, one of the bridesmaids at the wedding? Well, she moved in with George last year "ostensibly" to help look after his wife. It turned out that she had been in love with George since she was a teenager, but living in the same house with him opened her eyes to his real character and she walked out on him last week. I wonder who he'll persuade to be his chief cook, bottle-washer and bedmate now?"

The next day, Phyllis received a second letter from Red Deer, this time from George, saying that it was still out of the question for him to remarry at this time, but he would like her to move back to Red Deer so they could see each other more frequently. A smile spread itself over Phyllis's face and she chuckled quietly, briskly wiping the palms of her hands together as if to say "good riddance." She removed the wedding photograph from its frame, and tore it into shreds, tossing the scraps in the wastepaper basket, along with the crumpled letter.

"Once bitten, George," she said aloud, "twice shy."

Dinner at Eight

I remember reading somewhere recently that a well-known literary personage, whose name, regrettably, I no longer recall, had once described Becky Sharpe, the leading lady in Thackeray's novel, *Vanity Fair*, as "the Sir Edmund Hillary of her day." Becky was indeed a first class social climber, and as we know social climbing is a contact sport—everything depends on making the right contacts.

Once upon a time, it is not so long ago (certainly within my memory), there lived a lady in Ottawa who could have given Miss Becky Sharpe a run for her money. I shall call her Mrs. Boggs. She was a first class snob, who cultivated people with money and position. It so happened that Mrs. Boggs had a brother who was the complete opposite, and took delight in aggravating his sister by his behaviour and choice of companions. He lived a Bohemian existence in Montreal, but occasionally dropped in to visit his sister in Ottawa. She tolerated his company when none of her important acquaintances were there.

On one never-to-be-forgotten occasion, he arrived, unheralded, just when Mrs. Boggs had planned a very special dinner party for some people she wanted to impress. She did not disguise her irritation when her brother showed up, and told him under no uncertain terms that he was not welcome that evening.

"Oh, it's you!" she had exploded, "You could not have come at a worse time. Now be off with you." She stood at the door waiting until she was satisfied her brother really was leaving the premises.

Her irritation that evening was partly a result of her anxiety. That dinner was the opening salvo in her campaign to have her husband appointed to the Senate. The evening had to run smoothly. Two of the guests were senators, and it was imperative that they be impressed by her husband's urbane sophistication and social graces.

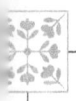

"Now for goodness sake, don't tell any of your silly jokes, and be sure to congratulate Senator O'Brien on winning the golf trophy," she told her husband.

She looked at her watch. "It's nearly eight; they should be here shortly. Make sure the fire is lit in the living room. I told Cook to serve dinner at 8:30 sharp, so don't offer more than two drinks or dinner will be ruined."

Eight o'clock came and went, then 8:05, 8:10 and 8:15, and still no sign of the guests. Mrs. Boggs was almost in a state of collapse.

"Where are they?" she wailed to her husband. "Are you sure you mailed the invitations?"

"Of course I mailed them. Do you think I'm an idiot?"

"That thought had occurred to me," she snapped.

Finally, as the clock struck 8:30, there was a knock at the door. Mrs. Boggs, not waiting for the maid, rushed to answer it. To her astonishment there was no one there.

She looked around and thought she saw her brother just disappearing into the shadows of an oak tree. Then she noticed that a large black funeral wreath had been attached to the knocker. Suddenly it all became clear, and she recognized her brother's fine hand in a cruel practical joke. In days gone by, when communication was not instantaneous, it was the custom to hang a black wreath on the front door to indicate a death in the family. Her brother had deliberately ruined her evening!

In a desperate attempt to salvage something from the wreck of the evening, she telephoned the one guest she considered a real friend and urged her to come over and enjoy the meal.

After Mrs. Boggs had assured her friend that all was well with everyone in her family, she explained that the wreath was someone's idea of a joke. Her friend was horrified. "How utterly tasteless! I hope you catch the culprit," said the worthy matron, "but I'm afraid we just can't come over. I've already taken my corset off and my husband and I are just tucking into a plate of bacon and eggs in the kitchen."

So ended Mrs. Boggs' campaign. Mr. Boggs never was appointed to the Senate, but perhaps that was no great loss to the nation.

The Tea Party

"**L**adies, may I have your attention please?" said Dorothea Doncaster, the elegantly coiffed and expensively clad wife of the Dean of Engineering, and President of the Faculty Wives' Club of the University. "Before I adjourn the meeting, I would like to remind you that our annual Christmas Tea Party, our final meeting for 1955, will be held on December 11, at 3:00 pm, here at the clubhouse. Are there any questions or comments?"

"Yes, Madam President, I have a suggestion to make," said Eloise Bennett, the Social Secretary. "I've noticed that Mrs. Irving, the wife of the new interim Dean of Agricultural Science, has not attended any of our meetings. I know she has been invited, but perhaps, being new to the university, she is unaware that she is entitled to full membership in our group. I think it would be a thoughtful gesture if someone telephoned and invited her to be guest of honour and pour the tea at our Christmas party."

"That's an excellent suggestion, Madam Secretary," replied Mrs. Doncaster. "Would you make a motion to that effect? Thank you. Seconded by Marion Morrison. All in favour? Passed! Eloise, will you take charge of inviting Mrs. Irving? Thank you. I shall leave the matter in your capable hands. The meeting is now adjourned. Light refreshments will now be served in the lounge."

"Has anyone here had a chance to meet Mrs. Irving?" inquired the President, addressing the ladies around her as they sipped their coffee.

"Well, I haven't met her yet," said one of the members slowly, "but I know someone who has. Apparently she is what one might call… unsophisticated. Now, I don't mean this to sound like a pejorative comment, but I believe she grew up on a farm near North Battleford, Saskatchewan. My friend tells me she's a real Westerner, in every sense of the word."

"What I've heard," said another member, "is that she's

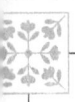

a practical, down-to-earth person, who does all her own housework. She and Professor Irving have five children, so she has little time to fuss about her appearance, or worry about having the latest hairstyle. I've also heard she's a real brain. When she graduated from the University of Saskatchewan, she had higher marks than the male student who was awarded the Rhodes Scholarship. At that time, of course, women were not eligible for those awards."

"I understand from my husband, the Dean," said Madam President, who was feeling somewhat uncomfortable about where the conversation was headed, and wanted to change the subject, "that it was considered a major coup, and a great honour for our university, and Canada as well, when Professor Irving accepted the interim appointment here. He could have gone anywhere in the world he wished—to Oxford, Cambridge, Yale or Harvard. There's a rumour that his name is being considered for a Nobel Prize this year. Wouldn't that be a feather in all our caps? So you see, ladies, it is very much in the university's interest, and indirectly ours as well, to have Dr. Irving settle here permanently. He has not yet made his decision, but I know I can count on all of you to make Mrs. Irving welcome in our midst. We want her to feel one of us, so to speak. By the way, everybody, Bella, our faithful kitchen helper, will not be on hand as usual this year to make the tea, and do the washing up afterwards, but we have someone lined up to replace her. I have to run now. Thank you all for coming. I'll see you at the tea party."

On the day of the tea, the ladies were all in a flap when the kitchen helper did not arrive at the appointed time. "Where on earth is that woman we hired?" ranted the convener, Mrs. Shaw. "She was told to be here at 2:30 sharp to get things ready." At that moment, the doorbell rang. She peeked out. "Good! Here she is now." "Come in," she said abruptly to the woman on the doorstep. "It's most inconvenient that you're late. You should have come in through the service entrance, but you're here now, so come in. Hang your coat there. I'll show you into the kitchen. Get the kettle on right away. Then take the cover off the sandwiches and cakes, and be sure to wash your hands well before you touch anything."

The newcomer obligingly complied. She rolled up her sleeves and went to work. The ladies on the committee busied themselves filling the milk jugs for the table, completely ignoring the new arrival. A short time later, the convener of the tea stormed into the kitchen, "I don't know what in the world can have happened to our guest of honour. It's nearly 3:10 now! We'll just have to start without Mrs. Irving. How rude of her to be late! Madeline says she'll pour until she arrives… if she gets here at all, that is!"

The figure bending over the sink, with the sleeves of her sweater rolled up, and a tea towel tucked into the waistband of her skirt, turned quickly and said in an apologetic tone of voice, "Oh! I'm sorry! I should have introduced myself when I arrived, but I thought you knew who I was. I didn't realize you were still waiting for me." Smiling, she wiped her wet hand on her plaid skirt, before extending it to the speaker. "Hello, everybody! I'm Pansy Irving."

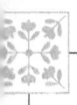

The Two Debbies

This is a personal reminiscence about my eldest daughter, Wendy Patrick, who died in 1989, and may explain why she had so many friends and is so warmly remembered by those who knew her.

It used to be the unfortunate practice, and almost verged on cruelty, for gym teachers to appoint two girls to be captains and allow them to choose their own team members, one by one, alternately. On this particular occasion in Grade 5, Wendy was chosen to be one of the captains and given first choice. Without a moment's hesitation, she called out the name Debby. There happened to be two Debbies in the class: Debby Simpkins, who was pretty, popular, and athletic, and always a first choice. The other was Debby Logan, who was overweight, shy and never anyone's first choice. Wendy had intended to have Debby Simpkins on her team.

Upon hearing the name Debby, Debby Logan, who was sitting at the front of the class, got to her feet with a surprised smile of delight. The girls around her were all saying "No, not you, Debby, she doesn't want *you*. She means the other Debby." Debby Logan looked crestfallen, then crushed, and slowly started to sit down again. Wendy, realizing her distress, said, "No, I did mean Debby Logan." There were gasps of disbelief from the crowd, as Debby, her face shining with pleasure, proudly took her place to stand behind Wendy.

I heard nothing of Debby Logan after Wendy finished elementary school. I was surprised, then, when I saw her at Wendy's memorial service thirty-five years later. She recounted this story to me and said she had never forgotten Wendy's tact, sympathy and the understanding she had shown, which Debby now realized was well beyond her years. She said that no one would ever be able to appreciate what Wendy's one small gesture of kindness had done for her self-esteem at a crucial period in her childhood. We cannot always appreciate the long-term consequences of a small gesture.

A Leap of Faith

I f she is alive today, there is a woman whose life intersected with mine in a uniquely personal way for a few brief hours on a day in late November in 1954. I have never known her name, but she has been an ever-present memory in my thoughts over the past 60 years. That day is engraved in my mind. This is the story of how fate brought us together.

It began with a telephone call from a friend who was a social worker in a family welfare agency.

"I have a favour to ask of you," she said. "I have a young Dutch woman in my office who sorely needs a helping hand. Would you be willing to see her and hear what she has to say?"

The woman who arrived on the doorstep later that day was about 18, tall and slim, pretty, fair-haired and neatly dressed. "My name is Gretchen," she said, in good but slightly-accented English.

She started by saying, "The first thing I have to tell you is that I am pregnant, and I am hoping to find a place to stay where I can work to earn my keep, doing housework or looking after children. I'm not asking for any money." She was very open and direct about her circumstances, and I took to her instantly.

I asked when the baby was due and she replied "In about six months' time." Prompted by a few leading questions from me, Gretchen's story gradually emerged.

She had a happy early childhood in Holland until her father decided to go off to fight in the Spanish Civil War. Although she did not understand what was happening, she vividly remembered her mother shouting, "Well, go off to the war then. But don't expect to find me waiting for you when you return." The little girl missed her father, and remembered how he used to carry her around on his shoulders. When he did return, he found another man living in their home with his

wife. He immediately took his leave of them and that was the last Gretchen saw of her father for many years.

Then out of the blue, in 1953, she received a letter from him from Canada. He had emigrated there and was now happily married to a widow with children. He had never forgotten Gretchen, and wrote to ask, now that she would have finished school, that she come out to stay with the family in Toronto for a few months, and accompany them on a winter holiday to Curacao, where they were going for some much-wanted sunshine after the Canadian winter. Gretchen had a wonderful, care-free time, made all the more enchanting by her charming and handsome nineteen year-old step-brother, Eric. However, she had the misfortune to fall in love with Eric, who took advantage of her adoration and innocence. After some months, she realized she was pregnant. When she informed Eric, he denied that he could be the father and made it clear that he would never consider marrying her. Not knowing what to do, she confessed to her father and step-mother. Her father was enraged, called her a tramp like her mother and literally threw her out, bag and baggage, onto the street. Her step-mother was more sympathetic, putting equal blame on her son, and gave Gretchen money to go to Montreal, and the name of a social worker at the family welfare agency, through which I made her acquaintance.

Gretchen blended right away into my family and soon became a favourite with my four young daughters. She was a great help around the house, willing to do whatever she was asked. She was always up early every morning, getting breakfast ready, and I became accustomed to the luxury of waking up to the wonderful smell of coffee brewing. One morning however, about five months after she arrived, there was no aroma of coffee, and when I got to the kitchen, no sign of activity. I knocked on Gretchen's door and found that she had gone into premature labour during the night, but had not wanted to disturb me. My husband was an obstetrician and would normally have been on hand to deliver the baby, but he

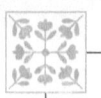

had gone to Toronto that weekend for the Grey Cup football game.

I phoned the hospital and the switchboard operator said, "Oh, just put her in a taxi." But it was too late. Gretchen couldn't walk and I could see the baby's head. I felt so helpless. What if something should happen to the baby? What if she didn't breathe?

There were seven doctors who lived on our street, and I tried phoning them all. None was at home. I was frantic. I wanted to rush out onto the street and scream for help. Fortunately, the baby virtually delivered herself, and by then, I had finally reached a good friend up the street who was a nurse. With a coat hastily pulled over her nightgown, she rushed down and arrived just in time to cut the cord and deal with the afterbirth. Using the first thing that came to hand, she tied the cord with the string from an Eaton's parcel that had been left at the front door that morning. I tried to pick up the baby, who was like a slippery eel, and she nearly slid out of my hands. I knew that I had to check that her mouth was free of mucus, and when she let out a cry, a huge sense of relief swept over me. Even thinking about it now, my heart starts to beat rapidly and my hands shake. It could have ended up so tragically.

I grabbed the first clean towel I could find, which happened to be a bright, garish shade of yellow. I still remember the baby's cute little face peeping out from that towel, like a rosebud that was just going to open. She was a tiny thing, probably only about five pounds. I then got a taxi to the hospital with Gretchen and the baby, leaving my friend the nurse to clean things up and keep an eye on my daughters who—when I realized the baby was on the way—I had placed in front of the television set, which was showing the Eaton's Santa Claus Parade, with the volume turned up loud.

"You poor little dear," I thought in the taxi, "whatever will become of you?" I almost wished I could have kept her myself. Upon our arrival at the hospital, two nurses in surgical

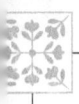

cap and gown, and gloved, rushed to claim the baby. I thought how their sterile attire was in such sharp contrast to the circumstances of the birth.

Gretchen put the baby up for adoption, but (as was common in those days) it was thought best that she should not know anything about the circumstances. I learned, however, from my friend at the social work agency that she had been adopted by a good and loving family who had the the means to provide her with everything she could need in life.

Gretchen stayed on with us for another six months, and often on Sunday afternoons, she would go to the Museum of Fine Arts on Sherbrooke Street, as she enjoyed looking at the paintings. On one of those days, I saw her escorted to our front door by a nice-looking young man. Gretchen explained that he was a McGill architecture student, a Ukrainian from Alberta, whom she had met on her visits to the gallery. Eventually, he proposed marriage to her and suggested that they move back to his hometown. Gretchen agreed and told me that, although she had been very happy in my home, she wanted to make a clean break and start a new life where no one knew of her past.

There have been times over the years when I have seen a young woman in Montreal who reminded me of Gretchen, and the thought has crossed my mind that she might be that baby. The memory of that dramatic episode comes flashing back, and I am startled to realize that she would now be over sixty. I cannot help but wonder how her life unfolded.

Evil Casts a Long Shadow

George Leeson refolded the newspaper he had been reading, slowly adjusted his bifocals and said to his wife, Ellen, who was sitting opposite him at the breakfast table, "When I first met you, didn't you know a woman by the name of Emilie Blanchette?"

"Yes, I did. She worked at the textile company with me," his wife replied, looking up from the section of the paper she was reading. "Is there something in the paper about her?"

"There is," said George. "She died. I'll read you the obituary."

> "On November 13, 1983, in Montreal, after a brief illness, the death occurred of Emilie Blanchette, widow of Eduard Blanchette of Paris, a distinguished member of the French Resistance, who was executed by the Nazis in 1945 and decorated posthumously by General DeGaulle for his outstanding contribution to the cause of freedom. Mrs. Blanchette, who was born in France in 1920, married Eduard Blanchette in 1939. She is survived by her son, Paul, with whom she emigrated to Canada after the war. She had a successful business career for many years, and was well-known in the fashion industry. A private funeral service will be held."

"Well," said Ellen thoughtfully, after a moment's silence, "I know it's not considered good form to speak ill of the dead, so it's probably unkind and uncharitable of me to say this, but I don't think many people will miss her. You know, I hadn't even thought of Emilie Blanchette in donkey's years. I remember hearing about how her husband was killed by the Nazis. She told me a long, garbled story one evening when she had had rather a lot to drink, about how she and her little son escaped the same fate. Her husband knew that if his identity were discovered, the Nazis would take reprisals against his family, and he spent every penny he possessed bribing an official to get his wife and baby out of the country before he was captured.

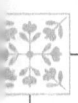

"Her son, Paul, was such an appealing little boy, and always so well-behaved. I used to baby-sit for him sometimes when Emilie was going out on the town. I was very fond of him. I kept him at my place for the weekend on several occasions. Another time I took him to the Santa Claus Parade, and once, on his birthday, which his mother had forgotten about, we went to the circus. He didn't get much in the way of tender loving care (or even attention) from her. I think the poor little fellow was so starved for affection that he latched on to me. Emilie was too self-absorbed with her own life to devote much time to him, even when she was at home. She shipped him off to a boarding school as soon as she possibly could, and dropped me like a stone once she no longer needed me to baby-sit. I didn't mind her writing me off, but I did care about losing touch with Paul. I had a soft spot in my heart for him. One thing I remember particularly was that he absolutely worshipped his father's memory, although he was only about three when his father was executed by the Gestapo. He was a serious little boy for his age, and was always asking questions about the war.

"Emilie used people shamelessly, and simply discarded them once they had served her purpose. Looking back, I don't think she had any close friends, certainly not female at any rate, although men seemed to find her irresistible. I worked with her for over a year, and spent a good deal of time with her, but I never really got to know her. There was something… well, for want of a better word, something… 'sinister' about her. I always had the feeling that Paul was afraid of her. I used to wonder whether she might have been a spy or a double agent during the war, or perhaps a 'closet' Nazi sympathizer.

"She was a beautiful woman, and had a kind of magnetism about her," Ellen continued reflectively, "and she knew it. I'm surprised she never remarried, although I'm sure it wasn't for lack of opportunity."

Try as she would that day, as she went about her daily routine, Ellen could not dismiss Emilie Blanchette and Paul from her thoughts. Late in the afternoon, on sudden impulse, she looked up his name in the telephone directory and dialed the number. A male voice answered almost immediately.

"Good afternoon," Ellen said hesitantly, "I am trying to contact Mr. Paul Blanchette. Do I have the right number?"

"Yes," said the voice, "I am Paul Blanchette."

"My name is Ellen Leeson. I don't know whether you will remember me or not. I knew you and your mother years ago when you lived on Sherbrooke Street. It was before I was married, and you would have known me as Ellen Cooper. I saw the announcement—"

"Ellen! Is it really you? Of course I remember you," the voice interrupted, excitedly. "I can't tell you how happy I am to hear your voice after all these years. How are you, and where are you?"

"I live here in Montreal with my husband, and I saw your mother's obituary in the paper this morning. I just want to express my sympathy to you."

"Thank you, Ellen. I appreciate that very much. As you may remember, my mother and I, to say the least, had a complex relationship. We were not close. I hope for her sake she is finally at peace."

There was silence for a few seconds as if he were mentally switching gears. Then, in a completely different tone of voice, he said, "Thank you for going to the trouble of finding me, Ellen. I can't begin to tell you how happy I am that you called and that we are in touch again. I've thought of you so often over the years, but didn't know how to reach you. I'll always remember how kind you were to me when I was a kid. As a matter of fact, you were the one bright spot in my life in those days. I still have the Swiss Army Knife you gave me for my birthday. It goes everywhere with me. You know, I wrote to you several times from boarding school. I didn't know your address, so I sent the letters care of my mother, but I guess she didn't forward them. I can't wait to see you. Would it be possible for us to have lunch together tomorrow? Yes? Well then, give me your address, and I'll pick you up at noon."

Ellen slept fitfully that night, tossing and turning, and by morning was beginning to regret that she had contacted Paul. George suggested she cancel the appointment and forget about the whole thing, but she was reluctant to do this. In the end, she was ready and waiting, albeit with some trepidation, at the appointed time.

The handsome young man who rang the doorbell had fair hair and blue eyes, and greeted her with exuberant warmth, throwing his arms around her and kissing her on both cheeks. He talked non-stop in the car, asking questions about her life and her family. Once seated in the restaurant, he reached across and took both her hands in his, and said earnestly, "I always wished you could have been my mother, but you know, Ellen, I feel that your coming back into my life is a good omen for the future. With your help, now that my mother has gone, perhaps I'll finally be able to get my life on track."

Over lunch, Ellen asked him about his life and work, and whether he was married. "No," he said slowly, "my mother took a sadistic pleasure in sabotaging any romantic relationships I had, even with the one girl I truly loved, and wanted to marry. I don't think I'll ever love anyone else in the same way again. To be honest, I don't expect ever to find true happiness in this life, but I keep busy with my work. I am researching and writing a book about the French Resistance in the Second World War, in which my father played such an important role. He was credited with saving the lives of an untold number of Allied airmen shot down over France. Just recently, I have been in touch with an elderly man, a former member of the Resistance, who knew my father well. He is almost certain that a woman who had a close connection with the SS was the one who betrayed him. He knows her name, but because there is no definitive proof, he says he can't tell me."

As they were leaving the restaurant, Paul suddenly said, "Would it be an imposition if I asked you to help me

dispose of my mother's effects? She always wore expensive clothes, and there are several boxes of jewelry and a couple of fur coats, as well, which could all be sold. I'd like to donate them to some charitable organization."

"Yes, of course! I'd be glad to help in any way I can," Ellen replied.

"Perhaps we could do that one day early next week," Paul said. "Tomorrow I'm going over to try to sort out my mother's steamer trunk, the one she brought from France. I don't know what's in it. It's padlocked, so I'll have to break it open. I think it's probably filled with old photographs and letters, and most of it will probably go straight into the garbage."

It was almost five o'clock when Ellen returned home. George took one look at her and said, "I'd say you've been through the wringer! Put your feet up, and I'll bring you something to boost your spirits." He returned in short order with a drink for her and one for him, settled down in an easy chair, and asked, "Well, how did it go?"

There was a pause while Ellen took a sip of her drink. "What can I tell you? It's a sad, sad story," she said slowly, "and I found it very depressing. He is a handsome, intelligent, well-educated young man, but he seems like a lonely, lost little boy."

"You have to remember he just lost his mother, Ellen. He's allowed to grieve."

"I don't think his sadness has anything all to do with her death. I think it all goes back to her treatment of him in his early years. I feel so sorry for him, and I feel guilty, as well, because I didn't try to help him. I don't know what I could have done, but I might have been able to make a difference. Incidentally, I told him I'd go to his mother's apartment with him in a few days, to help sort out the clothes he is donating to charity. I must say I'm not looking forward to it, but I feel I should do whatever I can to help. He's a very troubled young man."

Two days later, George, reading the paper at the

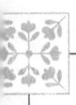

breakfast table, suddenly sat bolt upright in his chair. "Good Lord! No! I don't believe it! Ellen, what do you think has happened?"

"I've no idea," she replied. "Did I win the lottery?"

"No, I'm serious, Ellen! It says here that Paul Blanchette was found dead of a gunshot wound to the head in his Mother's apartment last night."

"What? Oh no, George! That's impossible! There must be some mistake. I spoke to him right after lunch yesterday. He was just going over to his mother's apartment to sort out her papers, and decide what to do with all her old photographs and letters. How awful!"

Shortly after nine o'clock, the Leesons' front door-bell rang. On the doorstep stood a uniformed police officer, who enquired from George whether Mrs. Ellen Leeson lived there, and on hearing that she did, asked if he might come in, as he had a letter to be delivered to her personally. Ellen, who was already in a state of shock, took the letter from him with trembling hands, and asked nervously, "Has this something to do with Paul Blanchette's death?"

"Yes, but I'm sorry I am not at liberty to discuss the case," replied the officer. "If you would please sign here, I'll be on my way." With that, he took his departure.

"Open it for me please, George. My hands are shaking too much. What do you suppose it's about?"

"We'll soon find out," he replied, as he slit the envelope open, and took the letter out.

"Read it out loud, will you please?"

George adjusted his glasses and cleared his throat. "It says," he began:

> *My dear Ellen, who was, alas, only so recently found, and now so soon to be lost to me!*
>
> *I am sorry to burden you with my problems, but there is no one else I can turn to. You will*

probably need permission from the police to use the key to my mother's apartment, which I will enclose in this envelope, so check with them before going there. I would like you to read the letters and newspaper clippings in the wooden box on top of my mother's desk, and look closely at the old photographs. I think these will be self-explanatory, and I know you will understand why I do not wish to live. It seems fitting somehow that I should use the same weapon to end my life as my father did. I am as much a coward as he was. Please forgive me for involving you in this unsavoury business. You will never know how much your kindness meant to a lonely child.

Paul

It was several days before Ellen received permission from the police to enter the apartment. When she and George went inside, they found it in perfect order. There was no sign that anything out of the ordinary had occurred there. Paul, it seemed, had thoughtfully taken the precaution of shooting himself in the bathtub, where his lifeless body, fully clothed, had been found by the building superintendent.

The wooden box was exactly where Paul had said it would be. The padlock had been carefully sawed off. George placed the box on the dining room table and opened the lid. Inside lay a Luger pistol, obviously placed there by the police after their investigation, and directly underneath it, the folded front page of a yellowing French newspaper, dated March 30, 1946, the headline of which George interpreted for Ellen. Translated, it read, "Former SS officer, Gunther Feldmeir, convicted of crimes against humanity, cheats justice by committing suicide." The accompanying photograph, dated May 1941, showed a handsome young man in the dress uniform of the SS. In a large manila envelope, there were a number of old photographs and snapshots, amongst them one

of a much younger Emilie holding a small baby, and standing behind her was the same SS officer in the newspaper clipping. There were no pictures, or any mention at all, of Emilie's husband, Eduard Blanchette.

Ellen and George examined the contents of the box carefully, and when they had finished, they sat back and looked at one another in silence for a few moments, as if trying to make sense of it all.

Ellen was the first to speak, "Poor Paul! On top of everything else that went wrong in his life, it must have been a terrible shock to find out his whole existence had been a lie. I can understand why he wanted to end his life. He felt he had nothing to live for. In his place, I think I might have done the same thing."

"I don't agree," said George, who was a practical man. "He was going through a bad patch, I admit, but he was young and healthy, and everything would probably have turned out all right in the end. I don't understand why he suddenly thought his entire life was a lie."

"Because it was, George! Don't you see? For the first time in his whole existence, he knew who he really was. He may have suspected it before, but he realized the truth the moment he saw the photograph in the wooden box. He had proof positive. He could see it with his own eyes. He was not, as he had always believed, the son of a hero of the Resistance, but the illegitimate son of a man convicted of crimes against humanity, and of a woman who had not only betrayed her country, but her husband as well."

"How do you know for sure that that's the truth?" questioned her husband.

You've never met Paul, so you wouldn't know," Ellen replied, "but here is the photograph of Feldmeir. The resemblance is unmistakable."

The Nun's Story

It has been said that everyone has three lives—a public life, a personal life and a secret life, and this story is a case in point.

The memorial service for Sister Angelica was held on May 3rd at the Convent Academy School where she had served as Principal, with great distinction, for many years. As two old friends sipped their tea afterwards, one remarked to the other, "What a wonderfully large turnout. It is a fitting tribute to a very remarkable woman. Margaret, you must be very proud of your cousin. I have been a staff member here under Sister Angelica's leadership for many years, so I know that she was an outstanding teacher, and established an excellent program here at the school, but more importantly, she was an inspiration to several generations of girls, and instilled in them a lifelong love of learning and a curiosity about the world. I remember there was one girl who was particularly close to Sister Angelica. There was a special bond between them and Sister Angelica encouraged her to achieve her highest potential, both academically and personally.

"She was so popular with the girls, she had such empathy with them," Frances sighed. "What a pity that she never had a daughter of her own. She would have made a wonderful mother."

Margaret was silent for a moment, as if considering whether or not to speak. She regarded her old friend, and finally, after a long pause, said quietly, "But the fact is, she did have a daughter."

Frances stared at Margaret in shock. "I'm astounded. I knew nothing about her personal life, even though the three of us were neighbours as children," said Frances. "She never spoke of it. I don't want to pry, but I would be interested to hear her story, as I had such great respect for her. I was particularly impressed by her religious conviction that gave her the special gift to be a powerful role model for the students.

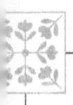

However, although is not common knowledge nowadays, I knew her religious zeal was that of the converted, as I remember that her family was not Catholic. I always wondered how she came to adopt the Catholic faith."

"She really was an extraordinary person," Margaret agreed. "When we were younger, we were quite close, and you know we were students at university together. It's amazing that she accomplished what she did later in life, considering the obstacles she had to overcome. She came from a dyed-in-the-wool Protestant family and only became a Catholic when she fell in love with a Catholic. Of course, you attended a different university from us, so you would not know the story. She was always well liked, but very shy. She did not have much of a social life and received very little attention from the opposite sex. She was, true to her name, a "plain Jane.""

"During the summer after graduation from university in 1941, she took a job at a large insurance company downtown, and met a young man named Peter, who worked in the actuarial department. He was very handsome—and personable, as well. He invited her out on a date, and they were soon "going steady." Never having had any attention from a man, she was completely swept off her feet, and assumed he felt the same way. Towards the end of their summer together, Jane, quite naturally, began to think about a possible engagement. Visions of bridesmaids and wedding bells danced in her head. Without intentionally doing so, she let slip to Peter that she felt they might have a future together. She was absolutely devastated when he said that although he was fond of her, his parents were devout Catholics and would never countenance his marriage to a Protestant.

"Soon after that, in the depths of despair and almost suicidal, on sudden impulse, she went into a local Catholic church and spoke to a young priest, Father Michael. He was a sympathetic listener, and after hearing her story, asked if she had thought of converting to Catholicism. By the time she left, half an hour later, she had made up her mind to take instruction in the Catholic faith, in the hope that this would make her an acceptable wife in the eyes of Peter's family. She said nothing of her plan to Peter or to her own parents, who would have been aghast at the idea."

Margaret continued the story, saying, "Jane began to look forward to the weekly instruction session with Father Michael and found herself relying more and more on his advice and support. She continued to see Peter and redoubled her efforts to keep their romance alive.

"The instruction period came to an end, and she was received into the Catholic Church in a private ceremony. She felt certain that the problem was resolved and that she and Peter would live happily ever after.

"Peter's reaction to the news of her conversion was utterly unexpected. He was furious that she had done this without telling him, and said that even as a convert, she would not be acceptable to his family. Further, he told her that he had just been offered a job in Vancouver and that as far as he was concerned, this was the end of their relationship.

"Jane was beside herself with despair and was unable to eat or sleep. She found it an effort to get through each day, and the nights were worse. In her anguish and despondency, she felt she had no one to turn to but Father Michael, and he became her confidante. He was deeply compassionate and suggested that the answer to her immediate problem might be to seek help from the Daughters of the Children of Mary. There she might find the peace and solace she was looking for. He thought that it might be the best place to go at this particular time, and made the arrangements for her. While there, she could reflect on her situation and perhaps consider the possibility of becoming a nun. Of course, all that her family knew was that, much to their dismay, she had converted to Catholicism and decided to enter a convent. I didn't hear anything more about her for another ten years. I don't know how she could have survived all that time in solitude and silence and almost total lack of human companionship. It was

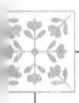

only by chance that I learned that after several years, she had left the convent and become Principal of this school. I arranged to meet with her and she told me that it was only her faith in God that had given her the strength to carry on.

"I have never told anyone this, but now that she has died, I have a feeling that perhaps Sister Angelica would like the truth to be known. Before she went into the convent, she confided in me that she was going to have a baby in March of the following year. The child was given up for adoption and quite by chance I discovered her identity, although as far as I know, Sister Angelica never did.

"I was at the hospital when the baby was born. Sister Angelica never saw her child, but I did. I also saw the couple who became the adoptive parents, when they were viewing the new baby. I knew who they were and I heard news of the girl from time to time over the years.

"Although the truth was known only to me, the irony is that the girl attended this school and was under her mother's influence and tutelage as she grew up. She is the girl you just mentioned, who shared the special bond with Sister Angelica."

"That's an extraordinary story. Have you thought of telling her who her real mother was?" Frances asked.

"I don't know if I have the right to divulge that information," Margaret said slowly. "It's not that simple. There are other people to be considered—her adoptive family, and then she might want to know who her real father is, and if he is still living. I'll have to think about it."

Margaret looked at her companion for a few minutes. "It's a moral dilemma, don't you think? What would you do, if you were in my place?"

The Young Pretender

The private lives of the rich and famous have always held a fascination for the general public, and any scandal in the royal family seems to be of particular interest. I am no exception to the rule, and cannot resist participating myself in a bit of gossip about royal misbehaviour.

On a summer's day in the 1960s, I was lunching with my old friend Don in the garden restaurant of the Ritz Carlton Hotel in Montreal. I noticed him gazing into the distance beyond my head. "Don't turn around now," he said, "but in a few minutes look behind you to your left." When I had done so, he asked me if I had had a good look at the face of the man sitting at the bar. I remarked that he looked very much like Edward, the Duke of Windsor, the former Prince of Wales.

Don nodded. "Well therein lies a tale. Would you be interested in hearing it?" I was all ears.

"When the very popular Prince of Wales visited Canada in the 1920s," Don began, "he was cheered by the masses and fêted by the establishment. What was not commonly known at the time was that he was quite the lady's man and carried on with a number of women during the trip. He was introduced to all the debutantes and took a fancy to a certain Mademoiselle R., the daughter of a prominent family. It was well known in certain circles," he said, "that they had an affair, and it was rumoured that she became pregnant."

Don continued, "But it wasn't until this chap appeared at the Ritz bar after the war that the gossip seemed true. He's never worked a day in his life and puts on airs. He's been living on credit here at the Ritz for years without paying his bills. Because of who he is, they don't say anything. He's always hanging around here at the bar, cadging free drinks. He seems to have no family ties or friends except for his drinking buddies."

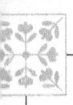

After lunch I dropped in on my mother and told her the fascinating tale. "That is a very interesting story," my mother replied, "but I know for a fact that it cannot be true."

"Why is that?" I questioned.

My mother smiled knowingly. "Because a good friend of mine was the nurse in attendance when that particular mademoiselle gave birth to an illegitimate baby, and it certainly was not the man you saw."

When I inquired who the father was, she continued. "He was never mentioned. Of course it was all very hush-hush, because the mother was unwed. The baby was a darling and my friend became very attached to the infant. An adoption was arranged for a lovely couple, and she kept in touch with them. In fact, they invited her to the christening." She paused, significantly. "One of the presents was a silver cup with a royal crest with three white ostrich feathers."

I asked my mother how she could be so certain then that the child was not the man I had seen at the Ritz, and she replied, "Because the baby was a girl!"

"Then who is the man at the Ritz, with that reputation and royal looks?" I wondered.

"Well," my mother retorted, "he may well be a royal bastard, but he's not Mademoiselle R's royal bastard!"

The Play's the Thing

"**H**elp! Help! My husband's trying to kill me," shrieked Lucinda Sanders, her piercing screams echoing eerily in the empty auditorium as a dark, menacing figure lunged towards her, brandishing a revolver. He seized her savagely by the hair, put the gun to her head, and was about to pull the trigger, when two brawny police officers burst on stage, guns at the ready.

"Okay, folks, that's a wrap for tonight!" shouted the director, hands cupped to his mouth. "Thanks everyone. Next rehearsal is Tuesday. Another stellar performance, Lucinda!" he said, giving her an enthusiastic, thumbs-up salute.

It was at that precise moment, and with the suddenness of a flash of lightning, that a powerful thought struck Lucinda, leading lady of the Brockston Little Theatre Guild, with the full force of a tropical tornado. What an absolutely brilliant idea, she thought to herself. Why had it never occurred to her before? It would be the perfect and final solution to the problem of Loring. Hey, presto! Abracadabra! Boring old Loring, as she customarily thought of her husband, when she thought of him at all, would be gone for good! Never again would she have to spend tedious evenings hearing how many paper clips he'd counted at the office that day. With Loring out of the way, she would not have long to wait for his aged, ailing, and wealthy father, already almost at death's door, to expire. Once the estate was settled, the loan sharks would be off her back, and her money worries would miraculously disappear. It was all so easy. Why had she waited so long to deal with the situation?

By the time she fell asleep that night, Lucinda had already conceived a plan of action. She had, in fact, devised two separate scenarios. If Plan A went awry, she had Plan B to fall back on. Unfortunately, both involved Bert Baxter. There was simply no way of pulling it off without his co-operation, and, as she knew, he would do anything for money,

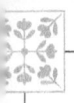

and there would be no shortage of that in her future. The following day, she set about bringing her plan to fruition.

Some weeks later, on an evening in May, a young woman by the name of Jennifer Thorne was watching the ten o'clock news.

"Turning now to matters of local interest," continued the TV newsreader, "an apparent domestic dispute ended in tragedy early this evening when police, answering a 911 call from a neighbour, shot and killed a fifty-year-old man. No further details are available at this time."

It took Jennifer a few seconds to absorb the full impact of the bulletin she had just heard. A fatal shooting here in Brockston by a police officer? Alarm bells began ringing in her head. Her husband Colin had recently been taken on staff as a rookie officer. It was unlikely, she tried hard to reassure herself, that Colin would have been involved in a shooting, but she could not dispel her growing anxiety as she waited for further details of the tragedy.

She listened intently as a car stopped in their driveway. It was only 10:20, too early for Colin, whose shift did not end until midnight. Who could be calling at this hour? She waited expectantly for the doorbell to ring. Instead, she heard the door open, then heavy footsteps in the hallway.

"Colin? Is that you? I just heard about that shooting on the news. I hope you weren't involved. What's wrong?" she asked in alarm as her husband staggered into the room and collapsed in the nearest armchair. His face was ashen.

"Are you okay, Colin?" Jennifer was instantly at his side, her hand on his shoulder. "What is it? What happened?"

"I...I just shot someone, Jennifer. I just killed an innocent man!" He slumped forward, head in his hands, elbows resting on his knees, his whole body reflecting shock.

"Good Lord, Colin! You shot and killed someone? How did it happen?"

"I...I really don't know. Honestly, I can't understand how it happened. Bert Baxter and I answered a domestic dispute call that came in from the neighbour next door. Our squad car just happened to be around the corner from that address when we received the call. The French doors to the living room were wide open, and we could hear a man shouting, and a woman screaming hysterically, 'Help! My husband's trying to kill me.' When we got inside, there was a man holding a woman by the hair and pointing a gun at her head.

"Bert immediately drew his gun, and since he was the senior officer, I followed suit. Just as I was drawing my gun, Bert stumbled and jostled my arm, and somehow my gun discharged. Suddenly the guy was writhing on the floor, blood spurting everywhere...I couldn't believe he was dead, Jen. It was surreal, like a nightmare, or a bad movie. I know my gun was pointed at him, but I swear to you I didn't pull the trigger. My gun just discharged when Bert jostled my arm, and the bullet probably ricocheted off the wall before it struck the victim. I just don't know how any of this could possibly have happened..."

Jennifer, who had been listening with a horrified expression on her face, interrupted him. "My God, Colin, how awful! No wonder you're in shock! What was Bert's reaction?"

"It was weird. He didn't even seem very concerned. I can't figure out what's up with him. I wonder whether he might be on drugs, or if he'd been drinking."

"Well, you're not in any condition to be analytical tonight," his wife said. "I'll bring you a Scotch and soda, and you try to get some sleep, darling. You'll think more clearly in the morning."

Colin was up well before daylight. Jennifer, who had slept fitfully, found him hunched over the kitchen table, looking as though he had not slept at all.

"I have to appear before the Inquiry Board at 9:00 am. What can I tell them, Jennifer? I keep going over and over the scene in my head, but something just doesn't add up. A piece of the puzzle is missing, and I don't know what it is. I think it

was something odd about Mrs. Sanders, but I can't remember."

It was nearly 6:00 pm when Colin returned from Headquarters. Jennifer saw at a glance that the day had not gone well.

He looked exhausted, his boyish face furrowed and drawn. He sipped the tea Jennifer brought him, and appeared deep in thought. Finally he looked up and said, "Did I tell you last night that Bert and I both drew our guns, and that he stumbled and jostled my arm just before my gun went off?" Jennifer nodded in assent.

"Well, that's not what he told the Inquiry Board this morning. He testified that I panicked, and over-reacted by drawing my gun, and that his gun was in its holster the entire time. He also denied that he'd stumbled and jostled my arm. I couldn't believe my ears! He testified to that under oath. Why would he lie about it?

"Anyway, the upshot is that I've been temporarily suspended from duty, and could be charged with reckless use of a firearm, or even manslaughter. The worst part, though, is that a man is dead, and I'm responsible. I'll never forget the look on the poor guy's face when my gun went off. The best word I can think of to describe his expression is 'surprised.' He looked totally dumb-founded. The neighbour who called 911 testified that Mrs. Sanders told her he'd recently started drinking heavily, and had threatened to kill her. You know, Jennifer, there's something about this whole thing that doesn't add up. Something I can't quite remember about last night. Something about Mrs. Sanders, I think."

The obituary notice, read as follows: "At his home in Brockston, the accidental death occurred of Loring Sanders, beloved husband of Lucinda, and only son of Alan Sanders. Funeral private. Donations in Loring's memory may be sent to the Brockston Little Theatre Guild."

Obituaries

Sanders, Loring, Brockston, ON
May 12, 2012

At his home in Brockston, the accidental death occurred of Loring Sanders, beloved husband of Lucinda, and only son of Alan Sanders. Funeral private. Donations in Loring's memory may be sent to the Brockston Little Theatre Guild.

The Inquiry dragged on interminably. Colin reiterated his testimony that Bert Baxter had drawn his gun first, and had stumbled against him just before the fatal shot was fired. Bert categorically denied both these statements, and his story was corroborated by none other Lucinda Sanders. Faced with such contradictory evidence, the Board was unable to reach a verdict. The Inquiry was adjourned until September, leaving Colin in limbo, his career on hold, and his life in shreds.

The stress of the investigation took its toll on Jennifer, as well as on Colin. If he were found guilty, even of accidental homicide, he might well be sent to prison. Jennifer could not sit idly by and allow this to happen. If there was an answer to this puzzle, she was determined to find it.

Jennifer had been concerned when Colin was initially assigned to work in tandem with Bert Baxter, whose unsavoury reputation as a womanizer was well-known, and whose integrity had several times been called into question during his time on the Vice Squad. She did not trust him. Convinced that he had lied to the Board of Inquiry, she set about learning as much as she could about his past.

Her job as a teacher at the Brockston Collegiate Institute gave her the opportunity to pursue her investigation during the long summer break. She had suspected from the outset that there was some connection between Lucinda and Bert, and that together they were up to no good. Both of them, under oath, had contradicted Colin's sworn testimony, and she knew that Colin was telling the truth. Was there some kind of sinister conspiracy between these two, and was Colin merely the fall guy who would take the blame?

A few weeks elapsed before her efforts bore fruit. She discovered there was indeed a connection between Lucinda and Bert Baxter. Both were members of the same athletic club, and had known each other for years. Jennifer's informant, an instructor at the club, reported he had twice seen them recently having a tête-à-tête at a bar in Montreal. He also happened to mention that Lucinda had already dispensed legally with two

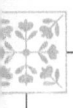

husbands before her marriage to Loring. Moreover, she was reputedly in debt to loan sharks up to her plucked eyebrows. All this was grist for Jennifer's mill.

The composite picture of Lucinda that emerged from Jennifer's inquiries was an unflattering portrait of a self-centred, scheming, unscrupulous woman, who shamelessly cultivated people, and subsequently discarded them when they were no longer of use to her. Like a bee going from blossom to blossom, she extracted the honey from them, and stung anyone who thwarted her plans.

The plot thickened further when Jennifer learned that Lucinda had once been an Executive Assistant to Loring's father, at that time a successful business tycoon. Rumour had it that she had married Loring solely because he was heir to a sizable fortune. It was no secret among her friends that she would have dispensed with him long ago, had she been able to do so without jeopardizing the fortune he would inherit when his father died. The old gentleman was now in failing health, reputedly kept alive thanks only to the tender ministrations of his long-time housekeeper, Mrs. Sharp, whom Lucinda loathed. Their intense dislike and mistrust of one another was mutual.

The pieces of the puzzle were beginning to fall into place, particularly when Colin suddenly remembered that on the night of the shooting he thought he had caught sight of something that looked like a bullet-proof vest just barely visible beneath Mrs. Sanders' housecoat. Jennifer was by now becoming more and more convinced that Lucinda, with malice aforethought and Bert Baxter as her accomplice, had conspired to bring about her husband's death, and that Colin was indeed the fall guy.

Lucinda had planned it down to the last detail and she had planted the first seed by confiding to her neighbour that Loring was drinking heavily, had threatened to kill her, and that she feared for her life. Somehow she had managed to trick her unsuspecting husband into playing a part in his own demise. The challenge was to find a way to prove it.

It was Jennifer who thought of a way to do it, and it happened quite by chance. During the spring term, her Grade 12 students had studied *Hamlet*, and while marking essays one evening in June, a direct quotation from the tragedy caught her eye. The words "The play's the thing wherein we'll catch the conscience of the King," almost leapt off the page at her. It took a moment for its significance to register. "Of course!" she exclaimed excitedly, whacking her forehead lightly with the palm of her hand, "That's it! The play's the thing."

Jennifer planned her strategy carefully. It involved writing and staging a one act drama entitled "The Play's the Thing," which would be entered in the annual Student Summer Theatre Festival. It was to be top secret. No one, other than members of the cast, would be permitted to attend rehearsals. If the idea worked, Colin would be home-free.

Her next step was to make an appointment with John Ritchie, Brockston's Chief of Police and to work out a plan to solve the mystery of Loring Sanders' death. She and the Chief spent several hours together until they were satisfied that they had covered all possibilities. The key, they decided, was in the play itself.

Invitations to the opening night of the Festival were extended to the local glitterati and to the leading lights of Brockston, including the Mayor, the City Councillors, the Chief of Police, and senior members of the Force. Lucinda, as president of the Little Theatre Guild, was invited to attend as Guest of Honour.

On opening night, accompanied by a galaxy of guests, Lucinda swept majestically into the theatre, timing her entrance for maximum dramatic effect, and was rewarded by a sustained burst of applause. It was a glittering, black tie affair, and she was in her element, at the very top of her form, smiling, waving, and bowing graciously to important people in the audience. She and her satellites were ushered to their seats with all the pomp and panache befitting her position, and they settled down to enjoy the performance.

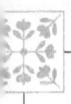

Enthroned front and centre in the place of honour, and seated next to Brockston's handsome, charismatic Chief of Police, Lucinda, fortified by several glasses of vintage champagne, allowed herself to indulge for a moment in the luxury of gloating. She had done it! She had pulled it off! She had gotten away with murder, and no one even suspected!

It had been expensive, of course, to pay Bert off, and there was always the danger of his blackmailing her, but, fortunately she would soon have her hands on a fortune. Despite the care lavished upon her father-in-law by his devoted housekeeper, Mrs. Sharp, he had conveniently expired, right on cue as it were, from the shock of Loring's sudden death. As the widow of his only son, Lucinda was the sole beneficiary of his will. Once the estate was settled, she could start anew, perhaps on an island in Greece, or in Monte Carlo. How cleverly she had managed everything!

The theatre lights dimmed. There was a sudden breathless hush, an almost palpable feeling of expectation as the curtain rose slowly to reveal the brightly-lit set. To the left of centre stage, a young woman in a housecoat, playbook in hand, rose and stretched languorously before addressing her opening lines to a man sprawled on a nearby sofa, clutching a cocktail glass.

"Darling," said the woman on stage, in a seductive tone of voice, "I've memorized my lines for tomorrow's rehearsal, but it would be an enormous help if you could just read the husband's part aloud for me. My leading man is hopeless. He shows no emotion whatsoever. I need to rehearse with someone more menacing, more convincing, so I can react appropriately."

The Chief of Police, Captain Ritchie, heard a sharp intake of breath. Lucinda was sitting bolt upright, rigid as though she had been electrocuted, and breathing heavily. He leaned towards her and whispered in her ear, "Just sit quietly for a few minutes, Mrs. Sanders, There's more to come. You wouldn't want to miss any of this, would you?" He slipped his arm through hers, and gripped it firmly as the performance continued.

"Try to make me feel you really *are* going to kill me." the woman said. "Now, after the part where I say, 'I want a divorce,' you read the next lines, threatening to blow my brains out if I leave you. Suddenly you go berserk and start shouting. Then you pull out a gun and point it at my head. I scream, 'Help! My husband's trying to kill me.'"

"Well, I'm no actor, but I'll do my best," replied the figure on the couch, amiably.

"Why don't you go and fix yourself another drink to help you relax?" the woman suggested. After her husband left the room, she pulled a cell phone out of her pocket–her housecoat opening enough to reveal a bullet-proof vest underneath. She dialled a number and spoke quickly and quietly, "All set, Bert, the 911 number should be coming in shortly."

At this point in the performance, Captain Ritchie heard an audible gasp from the seat next to his. Lucinda tried to get to her feet, but he was still holding her firmly by the arm, and whispered in her ear, "In a few minutes, just as the shooting starts, and before the lights come on, you and I are going to slip quietly out the side door, where a squad car is waiting. I'll escort you to Police Headquarters, where you will be charged with the murder of your husband. When I say, 'Now,' you stand up."

A few days later, at the Brockston Police Station, John Ritchie rose to greet Colin and Jennifer as they entered his office.

"Please sit down," he said. "I asked you to come here so I could fill you in on a few details, but first, I'd like to say, Colin, that you're off the hook. You've been reinstated. Congratulations! Secondly, it's thanks to you, Jennifer, that we were able to solve this case so quickly. It was a clever idea of yours to re-enact the murder scene.

"We were already suspicious of Mrs. Sanders, of

course, but after the re-enactment the other night, she realized the jig was up and confessed she'd planned the whole thing. She told us she got the idea from a play she was in! She made sure her husband had several drinks that evening. She asked the neighbour to call 911 if she ever heard anything suspicious, and she arranged for Bert Baxter and Colin to be close by in the squad car when the 911 call came in. She supplied the phoney starting pistol, and Bert borrowed one of our bullet-proof vests for her. They even rehearsed the scene beforehand.

"She told us if Plan A hadn't worked out, that is if the first stray bullet from Colin's gun hadn't killed her husband, Plan B involved Bert Baxter shooting him dead and claiming self-defence. Her motive, of course, was financial gain. As a matter of fact, she's hired a team of hot-shot lawyers to defend her, and she's been bragging that she can buy her way out of anything.

"Baxter cut a deal and told us the whole story. He claimed Lucinda blackmailed him into helping her get rid of Loring. I expect they'll both be charged with conspiracy to commit murder."

There was a pregnant pause. "I don't know," the Police Chief said in a conspiratorial tone, "whether you've heard the news about her father-in-law's will yet? No? Well, the delicious irony of this case is that the last laugh is on Mrs. Sanders.

"You see, in the end, her father-in-law's housekeeper, Mrs. Sharp, who is every bit as conniving as Lucinda, outwitted her. By having Loring killed, Lucinda played right into the woman's hands. Mrs. Sharp had kept the old fellow alive for years, probably for her own ulterior motives, and when he began to show signs of dementia, she saw her chance. She inveigled him into a secret marriage and had him change his will in her favour. As his legal wife, she inherits the entire estate. I can't wait to see the expression on Lucinda's face when she hears the news. Talk about just desserts!"

The Dish Best Served Cold

W arren Paterson was an enterprising and energetic young man, who, even as a teenager, exhibited a strong sense of upward mobility.

At the age of thirteen, he had a flourishing newspaper route. He was never even five minutes late with the delivery of the morning paper. He always placed it, neatly folded, in exactly the same spot on the doorstep, so that the recipient, who was as likely as not, to be in his bare feet and pyjamas, had only to open the door a crack and retrieve the paper without ever setting foot across the threshold. This was much appreciated by his clients, particularly on stormy, wintry mornings.

Most of Warren's customers appreciated his excellent service, and rewarded him by paying promptly when he called to collect on Friday evenings, usually giving him a generous tip as well...most of his customers, that is, but unfortunately, not all of them.

Warren had one subscriber who was a constant thorn in his flesh. If he happened to answer the door when Warren called to collect, he would say disagreeably. "Oh, no! Not you again! I'll pay you next week. I'm busy now," and slam the door in his face.

Warren would then have to make up the deficit out of his own pocket, and take his chances on collecting at a later date. The old skinflint would only pay up in full when the newspaper office threatened, as they did from time to time, to discontinue delivery.

This situation continued for over two years, and only came to a halt when the family left town, which they did without notifying Warren that they were moving, or giving a forwarding address, leaving an unpaid bill for $17.53, which Warren had to pay out of his own pocket. This sum represented a large part of his monthly earnings, and it taught

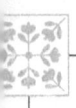

him a lesson he never forgot. He kept the unpaid bill in a scrapbook, just as a reminder, and the memory never failed to rankle whenever he thought of it. It was not so much the loss of the money that bothered him — it was the fact that behaviour such as that outraged the sense of moral values by which he lived.

Fast-forward twenty-five years. Warren Paterson, MBA, is now a top executive in a large financial institution, and lives with his wife and children in Vancouver. He is still the same conscientious person he was as a teenager. He has done extremely well in both his private life and in his business career.

It had been a long and unusually busy Friday at the office. It was now just after 4:00 pm. Warren checked his schedule, and since he had no more appointments, decided he might as well knock off early, as it was too late to start anything. He was about to turn off the computer when his executive assistant tapped on the door and entered.

"Warren," she said in a warning tone, rolling her eyes as she spoke, "there's a... an individual outside insisting he has to see you this afternoon."

"Who is he? Do you know him?" Warren inquired.

"No, but he gave me his name," she replied. "It's Vincent Gossage."

"Vincent Gossage! What does he want?" said Warren, surprised.

"He wouldn't say. He just kept insisting that he had to see you about an important business transaction."

"Just let him cool his heels out there for the next half hour, Beth. I'm going home now, but don't say I can't see him today till you're ready to leave at five o'clock. Then give him a fifteen-minute appointment for a week from next Tuesday. I'm going to slip out the back way now. Have a great weekend. See you Monday."

On the day of Vincent Gossage's appointment, Warren took extra care with his appearance. He wore his most expensive suit, a crisp white shirt, and his monogrammed gold cuff-links. He had instructed Beth to let Gossage wait for fifteen minutes before ushering him into the inner sanctum, and he deliberately waited a few extra minutes before looking up from his desk to acknowledge his presence.

He remained seated as Gossage entered. "Good morning," he said absent-mindedly, "What is your name again? Oh yes, Gossage. Gossage! It seems to me I've heard that name somewhere before. Now, what do you wish to see me about?"

"It's about a new business venture I'm contemplating. I decided I'd give your firm a chance to get in on the ground floor," said Gossage magnanimously. "I've brought all the information with me, and I can explain it to you right now. I know you'll want to get in on such a sure thing."

"Does this venture of yours have anything to do with borrowing money from our firm, Mr. Gossage?" interrupted Warren.

"Well, in a way it does," said Gossage, "but it would be an opportunity for your firm, and perhaps you yourself, to make some money on the q.t. I'm sure you and I can do business together." He winked conspiratorially.

Warren looked him straight in the eye. "I wouldn't do business with you, Gossage, if you were the last man alive. You don't remember me, do you? I was your paperboy when you lived in Montreal, and by the way, I have something for you. I've been saving it all these years." He opened his desk drawer and took out a slip of paper, which he handed to Gossage. "It's an unpaid account for $17.53, plus interest, compounded annually for the last twenty-six years. You can either pay me right now, or my lawyer will contact you, whichever you prefer."

Gossage's countenance reflected in turn, surprise, then embarrassment, then annoyance. However, he had the good sense to know that this particular scheme was a lost cause, and reluctantly pulled out his wallet and threw a bill on the desk. Warren had returned to studying the papers on his desk and did not look up. Gossage turned on his heel and left the room without a word.

Warren smiled as he tucked the money into his wallet. "Perhaps there is truth in the old saying that revenge is a dish best served cold."

In Dublin's Fair City

"The problem is, Jane," said Larry, "the guide book doesn't say how far Clongowes College is from here, but if we knew whether it was within walking distance, it would be a big help. Why don't I ask this old codger coming along here now? Maybe he can tell us."

"Excuse me, sir," the young man said, rising from the park bench, guide book in hand, and addressing the elderly gentleman, who, with the aid of a sturdy walking stick, was slowly making his way along the path. "Good morning to you, sir. Are you by any chance a native of Dublin?"

The old gentleman stopped in his tracks, and lowering his head slightly, regarded the young man solemnly for a moment from over the top of his spectacles before replying. "I am indeed, and top o' the morning to you! Can I be of any assistance to you and the young lady? I see by your guide book that you're tourists, and I hear by the sound of your voice that you're not local." His own accent was unmistakably that of Dublin.

"No, we're Canadians, sir. My name's Larry, and this is my wife, Jane. We're students at the University of Toronto, and we're here in Dublin for a few days to do research on James Joyce. What we'd like to know is whether Clongowes Wood College is near here?"

"Well now, Clongowes is a fair distance from here. You'd not be able to walk it," the old gentleman answered, smiling, as he extended his hand. "My name is McKenna, Paddy McKenna. Welcome to our fair city. Do you have some connection with Clongowes?"

"No, not really, except that we know Joyce was a student there, and we wanted to get a picture of it. I understand it's run by the Jesuits."

"Yes, and you're right, Joyce was primarily educated there. The Jesuits are skilled, you know, at instructing and molding youthful minds, but in this instance, despite their best

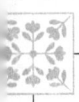

efforts, they weren't too successful in that regard with young Joyce. He had a brilliant mind, but like his father, he was violently anti-clerical. In the end, he completely rejected their religious teachings, left the Jesuits, and eventually completed his high school studies at Belvedere College."

"I gather you know a lot about him, Mr. McKenna. What kind of a background did he come from?" asked Jane. "Can you tell us anything about his early life?"

"Well, he had a difficult childhood, you know. His father, John Joyce, was a talented man, but reckless, indolent and irresponsible. He first made an unsuccessful foray into politics before obtaining a minor patronage appointment in the Civil Service, where it was said he applied himself diligently to doing as little work as he could get away with, and collecting his pension at the earliest possible date.

"After his marriage to May Murray, John Joyce continued to apply himself, again with great diligence, to fathering a large brood of children, only ten of whom survived infancy. James, who was born in 1882, was the eldest. His mother, worn out by too frequent childbearing and constant worry about money, died prematurely at age 44, by which time James was living in Paris. He had already made two unsuccessful attempts to study medicine, first in Dublin, and then again in Paris."

Mr. McKenna was warming to his subject, and obviously happy to have an audience. "You know," he said, "it's a fine morning for a stroll. If you like, I'll show you in your book where Clongowes College is, and you could go there another day. For now, I wonder if you would like to wander around the grounds of Trinity College and vicinity with me? I could give you a quick Cook's Tour, point out some of the interesting old buildings, and tell you what I know about Joyce and some of the famous people who studied here? By the way, you know that Joyce was never a student at Trinity. He attended University College, which was founded by Cardinal Newman in 1853, and later taken over by the Jesuits. Trinity is much older. It was founded in 1591 under Royal Charter by Queen Elizabeth I, and women have only been admitted as students since 1904. It only took a little more than three centuries for them to get around to that little detail."

"You're a walking, talking encyclopedia, Mr. McKenna," said Larry admiringly. "It was a stroke of pure luck that you came along when you did, and that I asked you about Clongowes. Is there anything you don't know about the life and times of James Joyce and the history of Trinity?"

Mr. McKenna laughed. "It's more likely that what I *don't* know would fill an encyclopedia, but the fact is that I spent nearly fifty years, my whole working life, at Trinity, and James Joyce, for some reason, has always intrigued me. As well, of course, I had access to many excellent books about him in the University Library."

The young couple's new-found friend proved indeed to be a veritable fountain of information. He talked almost non-stop, and usually in a non sequitur fashion, as well, but aware of their special interest in James Joyce, he sprinkled his conversation with amusing anecdotes about the Joyce family, as well as about his wife, Nora Barnacle. "I remember reading somewhere," he told them, "that when James' father heard he had run off with a girl named Barnacle, he was reputed to have quipped, 'Well, with a name like Barnacle, at least he can be sure she'll stick to him.' You know, do you, that although he had run away with her years earlier...I believe it was 1903 or 04, and they had two children, a boy and a girl, they were not legally married until 1931?

"By the way, I must tell you an amusing little anecdote of James' first day at Clongowes School. He was a precocious child, and the story is told that when asked by the Headmaster how old he was, he had replied solemnly, "Half past six, sir," and thereby established a reputation amongst his classmates as a bit of a wit."

Mr. McKenna was also a gold mine of information about Nora's life and background. He waxed positively

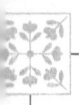

eloquent in her defense and in praise of her. "Much has been made, you know, of the social difference between James Joyce and Nora Barnacle," he told them, "but apart from his years of education, they were not so very different—one from the other. She was by no means a simple, ignorant, country lass. Don't believe it for a minute. That was just part of the popular myth that Joyce had run off with a chambermaid, who was said to be neither intellectually or socially his equal. The fact is that, although she left school at twelve years of age, and had worked at menial jobs, Nora Barnacle was far from simple. She was a Galway girl, street-smart beyond her years, and well able to take care of herself. Someone once described her as 'a pretty lass with a bright ribbon in her hair, and a sharp tongue in her head.' She was a witty, attractive, intelligent young woman, and her co-workers at Finn's Hotel regarded Joyce as merely an unemployed writer, best known for his consumption of liquor, and his inability to hold it. They were not impressed with him, and felt she could have done much better. The fact is that Nora was the spark that lit his genius. Without her, he might never have amounted to anything."

"Mr. McKenna," Jane asked, "would you mind if I make notes while you're talking? I don't want to forget any of the information you've been kind enough to share with us."

"Not in the least, young lady," he replied. "I am honoured to have such an attentive audience."

"Speaking of being honoured," said Larry, "there's a pub just across the road. Would you do us the honour of being our guest for a spot of lunch? We can continue our conversation inside, if we haven't tired you out."

"I'm not in the least tired," he retorted, "but now that I think about it, I'm beginning to feel a bit peckish."

The one-way conversation between the three of them continued across the table for over two hours. Larry and Jane listened with rapt attention. "Nora's mother," Mr. McKenna continued, "Annie Barnacle, threw her husband bodily out of the house when she had finally had enough of him. She was a staunch feminist, who refused to be intimidated either by her husband or her priest, or even the Pope and Catholic Church itself. She was in sharp contrast to Joyce's timid mother, May, who once confided to her priest that she was in very poor health and spirits, completely worn down by constant child-bearing, and she wanted his permission to live separately from her husband. The priest was angry, and sent her home with strict orders to fulfill her marital duty to her husband, and do penance for her sins. James' brother, Stanislaus, was furious when he heard about it, and later wrote, 'My mother ought to have rebelled, of course, but in the hateful time in which she lived, this would have required very considerable strength of character, which she did not possess.'

"In that context, one can understand what happened when Joyce died many years later in Switzerland. A Roman Catholic priest approached Nora, and offered to conduct a service of Christian burial for him. Nora was reported to have replied vehemently, "No! I would never do that to him!""

"We can't thank you enough, Mr. McKenna," said Larry, as they prepared to leave the pub. "I'll give you our address, and if you ever come to Toronto, the red carpet will be out for you."

"Yes, it certainly will," Jane chimed in. "You know, I feel I learned more about James Joyce from you today, than I learned in class during the whole last term. I can't wait to tell this story at home. Honestly, I don't know how we could have been so lucky, Mr. McKenna, to have been given not only a private guided tour of Trinity and Dublin, but, as well, a most interesting and informative lecture about Joyce, by a retired professor, no less, who by pure chance, just happened to be passing by us in the park."

Jane paused momentarily, and then said thoughtfully, "It just this moment occurred to me that we owe you an apology, sir. We should have been addressing you as Professor, or Doctor, not Mister, and you were too well-mannered to correct us. I'm so sorry, I just wasn't thinking. What degrees do you hold, sir?"

Mr. McKenna was staring at her with a bewildered expression on his face, and then he suddenly burst out laughing uproariously. "Oh, no," he chuckled, once he had caught his breath. "No, no! I wasn't a professor! The only degree I ever got was the third degree from the police when they thought I might be a member of the I.R.A. Although, come to think of it, my mates at Trinity gave me a mock bachelor's degree, just as a joke, when I retired from the Maintenance Staff after fifty years as Porter at the main building. I can't wait to tell my wife about this. Me, a professor? She'll get a real chortle out of that, I can tell you."

Author's note: The research for this story was done many years ago when the author was in a book club. The sources consulted have now been lost to posterity, so the author apologizes for any paraphrasing of uncited works or quotations. One book she does remember reading was *Nora: The Real Life of Molly Bloom* by Brenda Maddox, published in 1988 by Houghton Mifflin.

One Man's Trash

Driving home late one August afternoon, after a long, hot, mind-numbing day at the bank, inching slowly forward in an endless line of traffic, which stretched as far as the eye could see, Ross Morley made a sudden, life-altering decision. It was this: he would take early retirement from the firm where he had worked for the last thirty-five years. It seemed to him afterwards that the decision had been an involuntary one, something over which he had absolutely no control, as if an invisible hand had put his mind on automatic pilot. He was not even aware that he had been subconsciously thinking about the matter, but in the space of a split second, this momentous decision had been made.

It was totally out of character for him to behave in this manner. Normally he was cautious and prudent, and rarely acted on sudden impulse. Over the years, he had occasionally allowed himself the luxury of dreaming of early retirement, but it had never been anything more than just that, a dream, an impossible dream, and he knew it. Exactly what had triggered him to take such decisive action on the spur of the moment, he had not the slightest idea. Perhaps it was the fact that it was the eve of his sixtieth birthday, but, whatever the reason, his mind was irrevocably made up. Almost at once, he felt an immense weight had been lifted from his shoulders. He couldn't wait to tell his wife the good news.

"Janet," he called out the minute he stepped through the doorway, "where are you?"

"I'm right here," she answered from halfway down the staircase. "What's up?"

"Come and sit down and I'll tell you." Once she was seated, he said slowly, "What would you think if I were to tell you I've decided to take early retirement at the end of this month?"

Janet stared at him in disbelief for a few seconds, then,

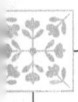

with a look of surprise and delight, clapped her hands together as a child might have done. "That's wonderful news, Ross, the best I've heard in years, but what made you decide at this particular time?"

"I honestly don't know," he began, slowly. "It wasn't as though I made a conscious decision to do it. I was stuck in traffic, and wasn't even thinking about anything in particular, when the idea just materialized out of nowhere. It was like spontaneous combustion.

"I can't tell you how relieved I feel, Janet, that my life will be my own again after all these years. It wasn't that I was unhappy working at the bank, but it wasn't fulfilling. What I'd really like to do before I'm too old is to buy a small farm, where we could grow our own food, or at least some of it, and perhaps have a few chickens, some sheep and maybe even a cow. I have very happy memories of the summers I spent on my grandparents' farm when I was a kid. My grandfather always said he was the luckiest man alive to be able to live off the land on his own little farm, and be his own boss. I think he was, too, and I always hoped I'd be able to do that one day. If it weren't for the fact that my grandparents' house burned to the ground not long after they died, I might have been able to buy it back again."

"Well, that would have been ideal," said Janet thoughtfully, "but now you'll be able to go wherever you want. It's a good thing we had our children early in our marriage. It was hard at the time, but now that they're both launched and financially independent, we can make our own plans without worrying about their future."

"That doesn't mean we won't have to watch our pennies," Ross interjected. "My pension will be a lot less than my salary was, but I'm sure we'll manage."

Ross lost no time putting his plan into action. Within a week he had given notice at the bank, and shortly thereafter all the documents were signed, and everything was in order for his retirement. By the end of the month he was officially retired, and received his first pension cheque. He had already contacted a real estate agent, and during the intervening weeks, he and Janet spent much of their spare time searching for a suitable property. Unfortunately, most of them were well beyond his means, and those he saw and could afford were either too isolated or too run-down even to consider. Ross was beginning to feel discouraged about the prospect of finding what he wanted, but was not yet willing to abandon his dream.

One morning, a few weeks after his retirement, a small ad in the local paper caught his eye. A fully-furnished, 35-acre farm was for sale!

He dialed the number, which turned out to be a local lawyer's office. The secretary suggested he pick up the key and view the property on his own. This arrangement suited him down to the ground. Armed with a roughly-drawn map, instructions on how to locate the property, and with high hopes, he and Janet set out.

Ross could hardly believe his eyes when he turned the key in the lock and entered the old farmhouse. Not only the front hallway, but, in fact, the whole house, was almost a replica of his grandparents' home, and had obviously been built at approximately the same time. Ross went from room to room in a nostalgic, trance-like state. Even the old furniture was similar, the oak dining room set with its press-back chairs, the mirrored oak hall-stand with its wrought-iron hooks, and the black horsehair sofa in the parlour, all were reminiscent of the happy days of his youth. Fortunately, Janet was almost as ecstatic about the house as he was, and went happily from room to room, mentally picturing how it would look with a fresh coat of paint. Ross was in seventh heaven, and had the uncanny feeling that the old house had almost been expecting

him. This was his impossible dream come true, and a small voice inside kept repeating that this was his destiny; almost, in a way, his heritage. He had to buy this property.

And buy it he did, that very day. Ross' offer on the property was immediately accepted by the lawyer acting on behalf of the estate and the transaction was completed in short order. Since the house was vacant, they had immediate occupancy.

Within a few weeks, they were comfortably and happily settled in their new home. Ross spent the first few winter months working on the interior, updating the kitchen, having a new bathroom installed, and refurbishing the parlour, dining room and bedrooms. When spring came, he ordered a dozen baby chicks, a rooster, and four sheep, and on the first mild day, he took his spade and started to dig a flower bed along the foundation at the front of the house. He soon discovered the soil was as hard as cement, and even a pick-axe made little impression on it. Beneath the top thin layer of soil laid a multitude of large stones, and this appeared to be the case everywhere he tried to dig on the property.

The question he was now beginning to ask himself was how he was ever going to grow anything at all on that stoney ground. Adding to his difficulties, Janet developed a severe allergy to feathers shortly after delivery of the chicks and rooster. This meant an end to their poultry plans. On top of all this, Ross realized a few days later that his well was running dry and would have to be deepened—a major and unexpected expense. All in all, Ross was beginning to think he might have been a bit hasty in buying the property. He made an appointment to consult the Provincial Agronomist in town, hoping to get an answer to some of his problems.

"So you're the fellow from Toronto who bought the old Parker property, are you?" said the agronomist, as they shook hands. "Well, that was your first mistake! You should have come to see me before you bought it, not after. You know the township isn't called 'Stoney Keppel' for nothing, don't you?

It's not suited for agriculture. It's all rock and stone! It would be fine if you just wanted a snug little house to live in, but if you need the farm to pay its own way, forget it." He quoted the old saying 'you can't get blood out of a stone,' laughing heartily.

Ross left that appointment utterly disheartened. Everything had gone wrong all at once. His plans were ruined and he was running short of money. In the town, he became the butt of good-natured joshing by his neighbours, who would ask if he thought he'd have a good crop of stones this year. Too late, he came to the realization that he had acted unwisely in buying the farm without getting good advice. He was almost ready to abandon his dream.

Sitting on the porch one afternoon, wondering what to say to his wife, Ross watched as a car drove slowly by, then stopped, reversed, and turned into the farm-yard driveway. The driver got out and strolled towards the house.

"Good day to you, sir," said the stranger. "My name's Morrison, Bill Morrison. I noticed as I was driving by that you've got some beautiful rocks here on your property. Mind if I have a closer look at them?"

"Not in the least. Be my guest," replied Ross pleasantly, "and if you feel like sitting here for awhile, you're welcome."

"Thank you, sir," said Bill. "I wouldn't mind taking a break. I'll just have a closer look at those rocks first." He went from one rock to another, and examined them carefully. "You've got some real beauties there! Would you have any interest in selling some of them?"

Ross smiled somewhat grimly. "I'd sell them all in a minute, if I were lucky enough to know anyone foolish enough to buy rocks or stones."

"Well now," said Bill, as he approached the porch, and sat down beside Ross, "maybe you and I can do business together. I own a construction firm in Toronto, and I can't get enough rocks and stones to satisfy the demand for stone houses, stone barbecues, and stone walls. My son runs a landscape gardening business, and he'd kill to get rocks like these. Everybody wants a rock garden these days. I tell you what! I'll buy as many truckloads as you want to sell me at the going rate in Toronto. I tell you, you're sitting on a goldmine here," he chortled.

Ross smiled to himself and mused, "As the old adage goes, 'one man's trash is indeed another man's treasure.'"

Western Hospitality

M y friends Molly and Joe were true-blue westerners—the real McCoy. One wintry Winnipeg Sunday, they drove to the airport to meet their friend Ben, who was arriving from Montreal on business. Spotting him on the escalator in conversation with a young man, they greeted him and were introduced to his companion, Doug, who, Ben said, was staying at the same hotel. "I told him you were driving me to the hotel and could give him a lift."

"Of course," said Molly, linking her arm companionably through Doug's, "but we're not taking you directly to the hotel. Dinner's ready at home, and Doug is most welcome. We'll drive you downtown afterwards."

"Oh, no! Thanks, anyway... I'll get a cab to the hotel," Doug protested, looking embarrassed.

"You will not!" replied Joe firmly. "You're coming home with us."

Molly had dinner on the table in no time; roast beef, Yorkshire pudding with all the trimmings, and apple pie for dessert. Afterwards they chatted amiably in front of the open fire.

Later, saying goodbye to Molly and Joe at the hotel, Doug said earnestly, "I've heard about western hospitality, but this was unbelievable. I've never seen anything like it. I don't know how to thank you for your kindness."

"Nonsense, Doug! Any friend of Ben's is a friend of ours," said Molly, giving him a motherly hug. "Now, you'll keep in touch, I hope. Be sure to let us know next time you're coming, and we'll meet you."

Early the next morning, Ben telephoned Molly and Joe. "Want to hear something funny?" he chortled. "That guy Doug was a complete stranger to me! He sat next to me on the plane and we got chatting. When we landed, he asked if I knew where the Winnipeg Inn was, and I said my friends were dropping me off there, and he could come too. He was only expecting a ride to the hotel, not the royal treatment you gave him. No wonder he was so impressed with western hospitality!"

Eeny, Meeny, Miney, Maybe
(A light-hearted look at life in the 21st century)

Everett Mortimer was a man who knew what he wanted, and given the fact that he was a multi-millionaire, he generally got whatever it was he happened to want at any particular time. As he approached his ninety-fourth birthday, what he wanted, or perhaps it would be more accurate to say what he fancied, was a twenty-eight-year-old ex-stripper and showgirl, who went by the improbable name of Candi Kane.

Acting on the premise that if 'a little bit of what you fancy does you good,' Mr. Mortimer reasoned that a little bit more of what had already done him good, would do him even better. Accordingly, to the horror of his family, his friends, and a host of legal advisors, he decided he would make Miss Candi Kane his lawful wife.

He was not in the least deterred by the difference in their ages, nor by the vociferous objections of his five adult children. He was deaf to all arguments, and so, without further ado, marry Miss Kane he did, in short order. Two weeks later, he expired — happily, it is to be hoped — leaving Candi the sole beneficiary of his estate.

The will, of course, was immediately contested by Everett's adult children. Candi was not overly concerned, particularly after she was able to negotiate a generous monthly allowance to tide her over in the interim. All she had to do was be patient for a few months. After all, hadn't Everett assured her the will was air-tight?

She took a short-term lease on a large, furnished house on one of the Thousand Islands and staffed it with a retinue of servitors, including a cook, gardener, house-boy and cleaning staff. She also kept a stable of young men at the ready; some of them former boyfriends, some of them drinking pals or just hangers-on. Now, it so happened that amongst this motley crew was a former doctor by the name of Chris Crawley (a.k.a.

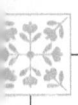

Creepy Crawley), who had been drummed out of the medical profession for unethical behaviour, and who now lived largely by his wits. He had been useful to Candi in the past, and now that she was about to inherit a fortune, she could be useful to him; he was therefore determined to maintain his relationship with her.

His crafty mind devised a scam, but unfortunately it was something he could not carry out alone. He needed a partner-in-crime to carry out his plan: a female partner.

"Dolly," he said to his girlfriend, in whose apartment he stayed when he was not in residence under Candi's roof on the island, "I've thought of a way we can make some easy money, a whole lot of it in fact, and you're welcome to come aboard if you're interested. The only thing is, I have to know for certain that you're in before I tell you the details. Are you game?"

"If there's money in it, count me in," replied Dolly without a moment's hesitation.

"Well, here's how it would work. I happen to know that Candi wants to have a baby, and it's just a question of time before she gets pregnant, either by me or one of her other stallions. I have a network of spies in her house, so I will hear about it almost immediately when she becomes pregnant. Once we are certain about it, you and I will conceive a baby ourselves. When Candi has the test to determine the sex of her baby, we'll do likewise. If they are both the same sex, we're home free! Are you with me so far?"

Dolly, who was not noted for her smarts, looked completely bewildered. "No! I don't get it," she replied.

"It doesn't matter whether you get it or not, Dolly," said Chris. "What matters is that you get pregnant on cue. You get your money when our baby's born." With that Dolly had to be content.

Chris lost no time putting his plan into action, and of course it was all made much easier by virtue of his medical background.

He soon had confirmation that Candi was pregnant, and so, in a short time, was Dolly. The tests done a few weeks later showed that both babies were male.

So far, so good, thought Chris to himself. Now all I have to do is keep Dolly out of sight and under the radar for the next few months.

In due course, Candi's son and heir was born, quickly followed on the same day, through a series of medical interventions performed by Chris, by Dolly's bouncing baby boy. The scene was now set for the denouement of his scheme.

There were, of course, a number of claimants to the title of paternity for Candi's son, all vying with one another, all jockeying for position, and all wanting a piece of the inheritance. Business was brisk amongst local bookies taking bets on the winner. Candi, ever the drama queen, enjoyed all the attention, and insisted that everyone who felt he might be in the running have a DNA test. She arranged to have her lawyer announce the results at a garden party to be held on the island. She even made up a little jingle for the occasion, "Eenie, meeny, miney, maybe, who's the father of my baby?"

It was a warm day, and the atmosphere at the party was tense. All the would-be fathers were understandably nervous. They each had a lot at stake, and only one of them could win the lottery.

However, Chris was relaxed and comfortable as they waited for Candi, the baby, and the lawyer to make an appearance. He stood a little apart from the others, happily contemplating his rosy future as father to the heir-apparent. His scheme had paid off in spades. His DNA test would prove conclusively that he was the father. Only he knew that he had switched the two babies at their birth. It had been a brilliant idea of his. It was absolutely fool-proof. This little fellow would be his meal ticket for the rest of his life.

At that moment, Candi, provocatively dressed and made up to the nines for the occasion, appeared on the veranda with the baby, the nurse maid and the lawyer in tow. There

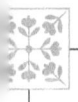

was a hushed silence and an air of expectation in the group.

The lawyer cleared his throat, adjusted his glasses, slit open the envelope and perused it for a moment before speaking. "This report," he announced, "was prepared and certified by the XYZ Laboratory, which vouches for its authenticity. There were several entries in this match for paternity title. The names of the contestants are as follows." He read them out slowly, then paused. "The father of this child is… none of the above."

There was a stunned silence. The lawyer continued.

"You see, Mrs. Mortimer opted to have artificial insemination, and the DNA of the donor is certified in this report. It matches none of the claimants, but it does match the DNA of the baby."

Chris gaped, open-mouthed, stunned, unable to believe what he had just heard. How could this have happened?

He turned to look at Dolly; she was openly laughing at his discomfort. What had gone wrong with his fool-proof plan? He was later to discover that after taking Chris' money, Dolly (with Candi's connivance and an appropriate reward), had switched the babies back to their real parents. As an old friend once remarked to me, "Dolly was not as green as she was cabbage-like!"

Candi was jubilant. She would not have to share the Mortimer millions with anyone else. She was still congratulating herself a few days later, when she received an official-looking letter.

Josephus, Josephus and Josephus
Barristers and Solicitors

Dear Ms. Kane,

With reference to the ongoing matter of the last will and testament of the late Mr. Everett Mortimer, which is presently in contention, it has been brought to our notice that on June 2, 2012, at which time you went through a service of matrimony with Mr. Mortimer, you were in fact still legally marriedto a Mr. Bert Billingsly Bennett of Ochre Pit Cove, Newfoundland. Our research shows that marriage was never legally dissolved.

Please be advised that Mr. Mortimer's will, in which he bequeathed his entire estate to his lawful wife, is therefore null and void, as you were never legally married to him. The monthly stipend you have been receiving will cease as of this date. You will also face legal action to recover the amount you have already received under false pretenses.

Yours faithfully,

George Josephus

George Josephus
Josephus, Josephus and Josephus
Barristers and Solicitors

Candi tossed the letter aside with a shrug. Ever the optimist, she mused, "Oh well, easy come, easy go," of her ill-gotten gain. "On to the next sucker." She was never at a loss for "Plan B" when it came to feathering her own nest. She had a fat file in her desk of wealthy elderly gents who would be easy prey.

"Candi"
Illustration by
Nancy Patrick, 1962

Afterward

As a nonagenarian, Bunty really had seen it all, from wireless radio operation to wireless internet access. In this collection of stories, we have been given a glimpse into the world of her past—a world where a devastating war challenged the rigid social norms of the day and became the defining feature of her generation.

The post-war world continued to push against social boundaries and open up new ways of behaviour and different life choices.

As she navigated through nine decades, Bunty bumped up against many of life's shoals and currents. She was a shrewd observer of characters and incidents, capturing them in her own words, interweaving fact and fiction, in stories told with humour and insight. We thank her for giving us all her unique perspective on her time and place in the world.

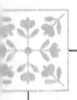

Praise for Bunty and her writing

"Nearly 50 years later, I still vividly recall the evening when, as a young recent immigrant, I sat at Bunty's dining room table listening to the stories of a colourful cast of characters, many of whom are depicted in these pages. One evening I laughed so hard that I had to be rushed up to Emergency at the Royal Victoria Hospital with a suspected heart attack! I trust that readers of Closing the Circle will not be similarly affected."

John Kellett, Bunty's son-in-law

"I met Bunty at St. Lawrence College in the 2000s, when we took courses in the writing of short stories. To the onlooker, she was always elegant, with an excellent sense for colour and style in her wardrobe and the most perfect manners. On the inside, she was gifted with an eye for creating beautiful paintings and the imagination for writing interesting-often mysterious-stories of a time before electronics governed our lives. I am glad to say that Bunty continued to contribute to the writing community despite her lack of eyesight in her final years."

Patricia Capitain, author, friend, co-founder (with Bunty) and chairperson of Writers' Ink

"Bunty's writing is a reflection of her varied and memorable life. She distills with remarkable skill tales of the past century with wit, wisdom and insight. Oh to have seen her in her glorious youth."

Carol Reesor, friend, art historian, author

"It is a pleasure to be reconnected to my youth on Strathcona Avenue, in Westmount, through Bunty's latest collection of short stories."

Joan (Moll) Kellett, close family friend

"The beauty and strength of Bunty's writing is her ability to have the reader feel a real connection to the characters and settings she is describing. What Grandma Moses was to painting, so Bunty is to the short story."

Jill Moll, close family friend

"Bunty's stories venture into some delicate personal situations, ethical questions and can dive into deep waters. They are full of surprises—poetic justice has a way of playing its trump hand."

Richard Keith Wolff, photographer, painter and filmmaker

"Bunty has been my mentor, muse and gateway to the world of good literature. I will treasure her book as a reminder of setting high standards in one's thinking and outputs."

Fred Pentney, friend and member of Writers' Ink

"Her stories glow with the sensibilities I've admired in her since I called her Aunt Bunty as a child: her wry humour at human foibles, her compassion and her abiding ability to see the best in others."

Heather Menzies, author, daughter of Bunty's friend Anne "Beaver" Bayne and longtime fan

Closing the Circle: Narratives of a Nonagenarian was set using the following fonts: Allura, Arabella, Cochin, Comic Sans, Courier, My Boyfriend's Handwriting, Fountain of Frenzy, Futura Std., Gloucester MT Extra Condensed, Helvetica, Monotype Corsiva, Nymphette, Porcelain, Richard Murray, Suilly la Tour, Sunshine In My Soul, Times and Woodtype Ornaments 1. It was laid out and designed in QuarkXPress 9, exported to Adobe Acrobat PDF and published using the website www.lulu.com. The book is perfect-bound using standard-quality, acid-free paper made from wood-based pulp. The inside pages are printed using black ink (no colour) and should last several hundred years in an optimal environment. Bunty's daughters each have a printed copy of the book and an electronic .pdf file. Preserving The Past, LLC will also retain a digital file. The digital file can also be found on www.lulu.com for ordering printed or electronic copies. It is advised to store an extra physical copy of the book and the digital file (on an external hard drive) in a safe place. Orders can be made by contacting info@preservethepast.com and on various online bookstores including www.barnesandnoble.com, www.amazon.com and www.lulu.com.

It has been an absolute pleasure working with the author and her family. I have the utmost respect for Bunty, Barbara, Nancy and Susy. The entire family is remarkably talented and notably gracious and each is an inspiration to me. Thank you for allowing me be a part of this process publishing Bunty's second book of short stories.

Taylor Whitney, Publisher

www.ingramcontent.com/pod-product-compliance
Lightning Source LLC
Chambersburg PA
CBHW050800250626
47155CB00005B/2155